LOVE
AND
FREINDSHIP
AND
OTHER
EARLY WORKS

LOVE AND FREINDSHIP AND OTHER EARLY WORKS

LOVE AND FRIENDSHIP, LADY SUSAN
AND OTHER EARLY WORKS A COLLECTION
OF JUVENILE WRITINGS

BY
JANE AUSTEN

Editor's Note: The author's
erratic spelling, punctuation
and capitalisations have
been retained.

CONTENTS

PART

1

LOVE AND FREINDSHIP

Deceived in Freindship and Betrayed in Love

LETTER the FIRST, From ISABEL to LAURA

How often, in answer to my repeated intreaties that you would give my Daughter a regular detail of the Misfortunes and Adventures of your Life, have you said, "No, my freind never will I comply with your request till I may be no longer in Danger of again experiencing such dreadful ones."

Surely that time is now at hand. You are this day 55. If a woman may ever be said to be in safety from the determined Perseverance of disagreeable Lovers and the cruel Persecutions of obstinate Fathers, surely it must be at such a time of Life.

Isabel

•

LETTER 2nd, LAURA to ISABEL

Altho' I cannot agree with you in supposing that I shall never again be exposed to Misfortunes as unmerited as those I have already experienced, yet to avoid the imputation of Obstinacy or ill-nature, I will gratify the curiosity of your daughter; and may the fortitude with which I have suffered the many afflictions of my past Life, prove to her a useful lesson for the support of those which may befall her in her own.

Laura

LETTER 3rd, LAURA to MARIANNE

As the Daughter of my most intimate freind I think you entitled to that knowledge of my unhappy story, which your Mother has so often solicited me to give you.

My Father was a native of Ireland and an inhabitant of Wales; my Mother was the natural Daughter of a Scotch Peer by an italian Opera-girl—I was born in Spain and received my Education at a Convent in France.

When I had reached my eighteenth Year I was recalled by my Parents to my paternal roof in Wales. Our mansion was situated in one of the most romantic parts of the Vale of Uske. Tho' my Charms are now considerably softened and somewhat impaired by the Misfortunes I have undergone, I was once beautiful. But lovely as I was the Graces of my Person were the least of my Perfections. Of every accomplishment accustomary to my sex, I was Mistress. When in the Convent, my progress had always exceeded my instructions, my Acquirements had been wonderfull for my age, and I had shortly surpassed my Masters.

In my Mind, every Virtue that could adorn it was centered; it was the Rendez-vous of every good Quality and of every noble sentiment.

A sensibility too tremblingly alive to every affliction of my Freinds, my Acquaintance and particularly to every affliction of my own, was my only fault, if a fault it could be called. Alas! how altered now! Tho' indeed my own Misfortunes do not make less impression on me than they ever did, yet now I never feel for those of an other. My accomplishments too, begin to fade—I can neither sing so well nor Dance so gracefully as I once did—and I have entirely forgot the MINUET DELA COUR.

Adeiu
Laura.

●

LETTER 4th, LAURA to MARIANNE

Our neighbourhood was small, for it consisted only of your Mother. She may probably have already told you that being left by her Parents in indigent Circumstances she had retired into Wales on eoconomical motives. There it was our

LOVE
AND
FREINDSHIP
AND
OTHER
EARLY
WORKS

freindship first commenced. Isobel was then one and twenty. Tho' pleasing both in her Person and Manners (between ourselves) she never possessed the hundredth part of my Beauty or Accomplishments. Isabel had seen the World. She had passed 2 Years at one of the first Boarding-schools in London; had spent a fortnight in Bath and had supped one night in Southampton.

"Beware my Laura (she would often say) Beware of the insipid Vanities and idle Dissipations of the Metropolis of England; Beware of the unmeaning Luxuries of Bath and of the stinking fish of Southampton."

"Alas! (exclaimed I) how am I to avoid those evils I shall never be exposed to? What probability is there of my ever tasting the Dissipations of London, the Luxuries of Bath, or the stinking Fish of Southampton? I who am doomed to waste my Days of Youth and Beauty in an humble Cottage in the Vale of Uske."

Ah! little did I then think I was ordained so soon to quit that humble Cottage for the Deceitfull Pleasures of the World.

Adeiu
Laura.

•

LETTER 5th, LAURA to MARIANNE

One Evening in December as my Father, my Mother and myself, were arranged in social converse round our Fireside, we were on a sudden greatly astonished, by hearing a violent knocking on the outward door of our rustic Cot.

My Father started—"What noise is that," (said he.) "It sounds like a loud rapping at the door"—(replied my Mother.) "It does indeed." (cried I.) "I am of your opinion; (said my Father) it certainly does appear to proceed from some uncommon violence exerted against our unoffending door." "Yes (exclaimed I) I cannot help thinking it must be somebody who knocks for admittance."

"That is another point (replied he;) We must not pretend to determine on what motive the person may knock—tho' that someone *does* rap at the door, I am partly convinced."

Here, a 2^d tremendous rap interrupted my Father in his

speech, and somewhat alarmed my Mother and me.

"Had we better not go and see who it is? (said she) the servants are out." "I think we had." (replied I.) "Certainly, (added my Father) by all means." "Shall we go now?" (said my Mother.) "The sooner the better." (answered he.) "Oh! let no time be lost" (cried I.)

A third more violent Rap than ever again assaulted our ears. "I am certain there is somebody knocking at the Door." (said my Mother.) "I think there must," (replied my Father) "I fancy the servants are returned; (said I) I think I hear Mary going to the Door." "I'm glad of it (cried my Father) for I long to know who it is."

I was right in my conjecture; for Mary instantly entering the Room, informed us that a young Gentleman and his Servant were at the door, who had lossed their way, were very cold and begged leave to warm themselves by our fire.

"Won't you admit them?" (said I.) "You have no objection, my Dear?" (said my Father.) "None in the World." (replied my Mother.)

Mary, without waiting for any further commands immediately left the room and quickly returned introducing the most beauteous and amiable Youth, I had ever beheld. The servant she kept to herself.

My natural sensibility had already been greatly affected by the sufferings of the unfortunate stranger and no sooner did I first behold him, than I felt that on him the happiness or Misery of my future Life must depend.

Adeiu
Laura.

●

LETTER 6th, LAURA to MARIANNE

The noble Youth informed us that his name was Lindsay—for particular reasons however I shall conceal it under that of Talbot. He told us that he was the son of an English Baronet, that his Mother had been for many years no more and that he had a Sister of the middle size. "My Father (he continued) is a mean and mercenary wretch—it is only to such particular freinds as this Dear Party that I would thus betray his failings. Your Virtues my amiable Polydore (addressing himself to my

LOVE
AND
FREINDSHIP
AND
OTHER
EARLY
WORKS

father) yours Dear Claudia and yours my Charming Laura call on me to repose in you, my confidence." We bowed. "My Father seduced by the false glare of Fortune and the Deluding Pomp of Title, insisted on my giving my hand to Lady Dorothea. No never exclaimed I. Lady Dorothea is lovely and Engaging; I prefer no woman to her; but know Sir, that I scorn to marry her in compliance with your Wishes. No! Never shall it be said that I obliged my Father."

We all admired the noble Manliness of his reply. He continued.

"Sir Edward was surprised; he had perhaps little expected to meet with so spirited an opposition to his will. "Where, Edward in the name of wonder (said he) did you pick up this unmeaning gibberish? You have been studying Novels I suspect." I scorned to answer: it would have been beneath my dignity. I mounted my Horse and followed by my faithful William set forth for my Aunts."

"My Father's house is situated in Bedfordshire, my Aunt's in Middlesex, and tho' I flatter myself with being a tolerable proficient in Geography, I know not how it happened, but I found myself entering this beautifull Vale which I find is in South Wales, when I had expected to have reached my Aunts."

"After having wandered some time on the Banks of the Uske without knowing which way to go, I began to lament my cruel Destiny in the bitterest and most pathetic Manner. It was now perfectly dark, not a single star was there to direct my steps, and I know not what might have befallen me had I not at length discerned thro' the solemn Gloom that surrounded me a distant light, which as I approached it, I discovered to be the chearfull Blaze of your fire. Impelled by the combination of Misfortunes under which I laboured, namely Fear, Cold and Hunger I hesitated not to ask admittance which at length I have gained; and now my Adorable Laura (continued he taking my Hand) when may I hope to receive that reward of all the painfull sufferings I have undergone during the course of my attachment to you, to which I have ever aspired. Oh! when will you reward me with Yourself?"

"This instant, Dear and Amiable Edward." (replied I.) We were immediately united by my Father, who tho' he had never taken orders had been bred to the Church.

Adeiu
Laura

●

LETTER 7th, LAURA to MARIANNE

We remained but a few days after our Marriage, in the Vale of Uske. After taking an affecting Farewell of my Father, my Mother and my Isabel, I accompanied Edward to his Aunt's in Middlesex. Philippa received us both with every expression of affectionate Love. My arrival was indeed a most agreable surprise to her as she had not only been totally ignorant of my Marriage with her Nephew, but had never even had the slightest idea of there being such a person in the World.

Augusta, the sister of Edward was on a visit to her when we arrived. I found her exactly what her Brother had described her to be—of the middle size. She received me with equal surprise though not with equal Cordiality, as Philippa. There was a disagreable coldness and Forbidding Reserve in her reception of me which was equally distressing and Unexpected. None of that interesting Sensibility or amiable simpathy in her manners and Address to me when we first met which should have distinguished our introduction to each other. Her Language was neither warm, nor affectionate, her expressions of regard were neither animated nor cordial; her arms were not opened to receive me to her Heart, tho' my own were extended to press her to mine.

A short Conversation between Augusta and her Brother, which I accidentally overheard encreased my dislike to her, and convinced me that her Heart was no more formed for the soft ties of Love than for the endearing intercourse of Freindship.

"But do you think that my Father will ever be reconciled to this imprudent connection?" (said Augusta.)

"Augusta (replied the noble Youth) I thought you had a better opinion of me, than to imagine I would so abjectly degrade myself as to consider my Father's Concurrence in any of my affairs, either of Consequence or concern to me. Tell me Augusta with sincerity; did you ever know me consult his inclinations or follow his Advice in the least trifling Particular since the age of fifteen?"

"Edward (replied she) you are surely too diffident in your own praise. Since you were fifteen only! My Dear Brother since you were five years old, I entirely acquit you of ever having willingly contributed to the satisfaction of your Father.

LOVE
AND
FREINDSHIP
AND
OTHER
EARLY
WORKS

But still I am not without apprehensions of your being shortly obliged to degrade yourself in your own eyes by seeking a support for your wife in the Generosity of Sir Edward."

"Never, never Augusta will I so demean myself. (said Edward). Support! What support will Laura want which she can receive from him?"

"Only those very insignificant ones of Victuals and Drink." (answered she.)

"Victuals and Drink! (replied my Husband in a most nobly contemptuous Manner) and dost thou then imagine that there is no other support for an exalted mind (such as is my Laura's) than the mean and indelicate employment of Eating and Drinking?"

"None that I know of, so efficacious." (returned Augusta).

"And did you then never feel the pleasing Pangs of Love, Augusta? (replied my Edward). Does it appear impossible to your vile and corrupted Palate, to exist on Love? Can you not conceive the Luxury of living in every distress that Poverty can inflict, with the object of your tenderest affection?"

"You are too ridiculous (said Augusta) to argue with; perhaps however you may in time be convinced that . . ."

Here I was prevented from hearing the remainder of her speech, by the appearance of a very Handsome young Woman, who was ushured into the Room at the Door of which I had been listening. On hearing her announced by the Name of "Lady Dorothea", I instantly quitted my Post and followed her into the Parlour, for I well remembered that she was the Lady, proposed as a Wife for my Edward by the Cruel and Unrelenting Baronet.

Altho' Lady Dorothea's visit was nominally to Philippa and Augusta, yet I have some reason to imagine that (acquainted with the Marriage and arrival of Edward) to see me was a principal motive to it.

I soon perceived that tho' Lovely and Elegant in her Person and tho' Easy and Polite in her Address, she was of that inferior order of Beings with regard to Delicate Feeling, tender Sentiments, and refined Sensibility, of which Augusta was one.

She staid but half an hour and neither in the Course of her Visit, confided to me any of her secret thoughts, nor requested me to confide in her, any of Mine. You will easily imagine therefore my Dear Marianne that I could not feel any ardent affection or very sincere Attachment for Lady Dorothea.

Adeiu
Laura.

●

LETTER 8th, LAURA to MARIANNE, in continuation

Lady Dorothea had not left us long before another visitor as unexpected a one as her Ladyship, was announced. It was Sir Edward, who informed by Augusta of her Brother's marriage, came doubtless to reproach him for having dared to unite himself to me without his Knowledge. But Edward foreseeing his design, approached him with heroic fortitude as soon as he entered the Room, and addressed him in the following Manner.

"Sir Edward, I know the motive of your Journey here—You come with the base Design of reproaching me for having entered into an indissoluble engagement with my Laura without your Consent. But Sir, I glory in the Act—. It is my greatest boast that I have incurred the displeasure of my Father!"

So saying, he took my hand and whilst Sir Edward, Philippa, and Augusta were doubtless reflecting with admiration on his undaunted Bravery, led me from the Parlour to his Father's Carriage which yet remained at the Door and in which we were instantly conveyed from the pursuit of Sir Edward.

The Postilions had at first received orders only to take the London road; as soon as we had sufficiently reflected However, we ordered them to Drive to M——. the seat of Edward's most particular freind, which was but a few miles distant.

At M——. we arrived in a few hours; and on sending in our names were immediately admitted to Sophia, the Wife of Edward's freind. After having been deprived during the course of 3 weeks of a real freind (for such I term your Mother) imagine my transports at beholding one, most truly worthy of the Name. Sophia was rather above the middle size; most elegantly formed. A soft languor spread over her lovely features, but increased their Beauty—. It was the Charectarestic of her Mind—. She was all sensibility and Feeling. We flew into each others arms and after having

LOVE
AND
FREINDSHIP
AND
OTHER
EARLY
WORKS

exchanged vows of mutual Freindship for the rest of our Lives, instantly unfolded to each other the most inward secrets of our Hearts—. We were interrupted in the delightfull Employment by the entrance of Augustus, (Edward's freind) who was just returned from a solitary ramble.

Never did I see such an affecting Scene as was the meeting of Edward and Augustus.

"My Life! my Soul!" (exclaimed the former) "My adorable angel!" (replied the latter) as they flew into each other's arms. It was too pathetic for the feelings of Sophia and myself—We fainted alternately on a sofa.

Adeiu
Laura.

•

LETTER the 9th, From the SAME to the SAME

Towards the close of the day we received the following Letter from Philippa.

"Sir Edward is greatly incensed by your abrupt departure; he has taken back Augusta to Bedfordshire. Much as I wish to enjoy again your charming society, I cannot determine to snatch you from that, of such dear and deserving Freinds— When your Visit to them is terminated, I trust you will return to the arms of your Philippa."

We returned a suitable answer to this affectionate Note and after thanking her for her kind invitation assured her that we would certainly avail ourselves of it, whenever we might have no other place to go to. Tho' certainly nothing could to any reasonable Being, have appeared more satisfactory, than so gratefull a reply to her invitation, yet I know not how it was, but she was certainly capricious enough to be displeased with our behaviour and in a few weeks after, either to revenge our Conduct, or relieve her own solitude, married a young and illiterate Fortune-hunter. This imprudent step (tho' we were sensible that it would probably deprive us of that fortune which Philippa had ever taught us to expect) could not on our own accounts, excite from our exalted minds a single sigh; yet fearfull lest it might prove a source of endless misery to the deluded Bride, our trembling Sensibility was greatly affected when we were first informed of the Event. The affectionate

Entreaties of Augustus and Sophia that we would for ever consider their House as our Home, easily prevailed on us to determine never more to leave them, In the society of my Edward and this Amiable Pair, I passed the happiest moments of my Life; Our time was most delightfully spent, in mutual Protestations of Freindship, and in vows of unalterable Love, in which we were secure from being interrupted, by intruding and disagreable Visitors, as Augustus and Sophia had on their first Entrance in the Neighbourhood, taken due care to inform the surrounding Families, that as their happiness centered wholly in themselves, they wished for no other society. But alas! my Dear Marianne such Happiness as I then enjoyed was too perfect to be lasting. A most severe and unexpected Blow at once destroyed every sensation of Pleasure. Convinced as you must be from what I have already told you concerning Augustus and Sophia, that there never were a happier Couple, I need not I imagine, inform you that their union had been contrary to the inclinations of their Cruel and Mercenery Parents; who had vainly endeavoured with obstinate Perseverance to force them into a Marriage with those whom they had ever abhorred; but with a Heroic Fortitude worthy to be related and admired, they had both, constantly refused to submit to such despotic Power.

After having so nobly disentangled themselves from the shackles of Parental Authority, by a Clandestine Marriage, they were determined never to forfeit the good opinion they had gained in the World, in so doing, by accepting any proposals of reconciliation that might be offered them by their Fathers—to this farther tryal of their noble independance however they never were exposed.

They had been married but a few months when our visit to them commenced during which time they had been amply supported by a considerable sum of money which Augustus had gracefully purloined from his unworthy father's Escritoire, a few days before his union with Sophia.

By our arrival their Expenses were considerably encreased tho' their means for supplying them were then nearly exhausted. But they, Exalted Creatures! scorned to reflect a moment on their pecuniary Distresses and would have blushed at the idea of paying their Debts.—Alas! what was their Reward for such disinterested Behaviour! The beautifull Augustus was arrested and we were all undone. Such perfidious Treachery in the merciless perpetrators of the Deed

LOVE
AND
FREINDSHIP
AND
OTHER
EARLY
WORKS

will shock your gentle nature Dearest Marianne as much as it then affected the Delicate sensibility of Edward, Sophia, your Laura, and of Augustus himself. To compleat such unparalelled Barbarity we were informed that an Execution in the House would shortly take place. Ah! what could we do but what we did! We sighed and fainted on the sofa.

Adeiu
Laura.

•

LETTER 10th, LAURA in continuation

When we were somewhat recovered from the overpowering Effusions of our grief, Edward desired that we would consider what was the most prudent step to be taken in our unhappy situation while he repaired to his imprisoned freind to lament over his misfortunes. We promised that we would, and he set forwards on his journey to Town. During his absence we faithfully complied with his Desire and after the most mature Deliberation, at length agreed that the best thing we could do was to leave the House; of which we every moment expected the officers of Justice to take possession. We waited therefore with the greatest impatience, for the return of Edward in order to impart to him the result of our Deliberations. But no Edward appeared. In vain did we count the tedious moments of his absence—in vain did we weep—in vain even did we sigh— no Edward returned—. This was too cruel, too unexpected a Blow to our Gentle Sensibility—we could not support it—we could only faint. At length collecting all the Resolution I was Mistress of, I arose and after packing up some necessary apparel for Sophia and myself, I dragged her to a Carriage I had ordered and we instantly set out for London. As the Habitation of Augustus was within twelve miles of Town, it was not long e'er we arrived there, and no sooner had we entered Holboun than letting down one of the Front Glasses I enquired of every decent-looking Person that we passed "If they had seen my Edward?"

But as we drove too rapidly to allow them to answer my repeated Enquiries, I gained little, or indeed, no information concerning him. "Where am I to drive?" said the Postilion. "To Newgate Gentle Youth (replied I), to see Augustus." "Oh!

no, no, (exclaimed Sophia) I cannot go to Newgate; I shall not be able to support the sight of my Augustus in so cruel a confinement—my feelings are sufficiently shocked by the *recital*, of his Distress, but to behold it will overpower my Sensibility." As I perfectly agreed with her in the Justice of her Sentiments the Postilion was instantly directed to return into the Country. You may perhaps have been somewhat surprised my Dearest Marianne, that in the Distress I then endured, destitute of any support, and unprovided with any Habitation, I should never once have remembered my Father and Mother or my paternal Cottage in the Vale of Uske. To account for this seeming forgetfullness I must inform you of a trifling circumstance concerning them which I have as yet never mentioned. The death of my Parents a few weeks after my Departure, is the circumstance I allude to. By their decease I became the lawfull Inheritress of their House and Fortune. But alas! the House had never been their own and their Fortune had only been an Annuity on their own Lives. Such is the Depravity of the World! To your Mother I should have returned with Pleasure, should have been happy to have introduced to her, my charming Sophia and should with Chearfullness have passed the remainder of my Life in their dear Society in the Vale of Uske, had not one obstacle to the execution of so agreable a scheme, intervened; which was the Marriage and Removal of your Mother to a distant part of Ireland.

Adeiu
Laura.

●

LETTER 11th, LAURA in continuation

"I have a Relation in Scotland (said Sophia to me as we left London) who I am certain would not hesitate in receiving me." "Shall I order the Boy to drive there?" said I—but instantly recollecting myself, exclaimed, "Alas I fear it will be too long a Journey for the Horses." Unwilling however to act only from my own inadequate Knowledge of the Strength and Abilities of Horses, I consulted the Postilion, who was entirely of my Opinion concerning the Affair. We therefore determined to change Horses at the next Town and to travel Post the remainder of the Journey—. When we arrived at the last Inn

LOVE
AND
FREINDSHIP
AND
OTHER
EARLY
WORKS

we were to stop at, which was but a few miles from the House of Sophia's Relation, unwilling to intrude our Society on him unexpected and unthought of, we wrote a very elegant and well penned Note to him containing an account of our Destitute and melancholy Situation, and of our intention to spend some months with him in Scotland. As soon as we had dispatched this Letter, we immediately prepared to follow it in person and were stepping into the Carriage for that Purpose when our attention was attracted by the Entrance of a coroneted Coach and 4 into the Inn-yard. A Gentleman considerably advanced in years descended from it. At his first Appearance my Sensibility was wonderfully affected and e'er I had gazed at him a 2d time, an instinctive sympathy whispered to my Heart, that he was my Grandfather. Convinced that I could not be mistaken in my conjecture I instantly sprang from the Carriage I had just entered, and following the Venerable Stranger into the Room he had been shewn to, I threw myself on my knees before him and besought him to acknowledge me as his Grand Child. He started, and having attentively examined my features, raised me from the Ground and throwing his Grand-fatherly arms around my Neck, exclaimed, "Acknowledge thee! Yes dear resemblance of my Laurina and Laurina's Daughter, sweet image of my Claudia and my Claudia's Mother, I do acknowledge thee as the Daughter of the one and the Grandaughter of the other." While he was thus tenderly embracing me, Sophia astonished at my precipitate Departure, entered the Room in search of me. No sooner had she caught the eye of the venerable Peer, than he exclaimed with every mark of Astonishment— "Another Grandaughter! Yes, yes, I see you are the Daughter of my Laurina's eldest Girl; your resemblance to the beauteous Matilda sufficiently proclaims it. "Oh!" replied Sophia, "when I first beheld you the instinct of Nature whispered me that we were in some degree related—But whether Grandfathers, or Grandmothers, I could not pretend to determine." He folded her in his arms, and whilst they were tenderly embracing, the Door of the Apartment opened and a most beautifull young Man appeared. On perceiving him Lord St. Clair started and retreating back a few paces, with uplifted Hands, said, "Another Grand-child! What an unexpected Happiness is this! to discover in the space of 3 minutes, as many of my Descendants! This I am certain is Philander the son of my Laurina's 3d girl the amiable Bertha; there wants now but the presence of Gustavus to compleat the Union of my Laurina's Grand-Children."

"And here he is; (said a Gracefull Youth who that instant entered the room) here is the Gustavus you desire to see. I am the son of Agatha your Laurina's 4th and youngest Daughter," "I see you are indeed; replied Lord St. Clair—But tell me (continued he looking fearfully towards the Door) tell me, have I any other Grand-children in the House." "None my Lord." "Then I will provide for you all without farther delay—Here are 4 Banknotes of 50L each—Take them and remember I have done the Duty of a Grandfather." He instantly left the Room and immediately afterwards the House.

Adeiu,
Laura.

•

LETTER the 12th, LAURA in continuation

You may imagine how greatly we were surprised by the sudden departure of Lord St Clair. "Ignoble Grand-sire!" exclaimed Sophia. "Unworthy Grandfather!" said I, and instantly fainted in each other's arms. How long we remained in this situation I know not; but when we recovered we found ourselves alone, without either Gustavus, Philander, or the Banknotes. As we were deploring our unhappy fate, the Door of the Apartment opened and "Macdonald" was announced. He was Sophia's cousin. The haste with which he came to our releif so soon after the receipt of our Note, spoke so greatly in his favour that I hesitated not to pronounce him at first sight, a tender and simpathetic Freind. Alas! he little deserved the name—for though he told us that he was much concerned at our Misfortunes, yet by his own account it appeared that the perusal of them, had neither drawn from him a single sigh, nor induced him to bestow one curse on our vindictive stars—. He told Sophia that his Daughter depended on her returning with him to Macdonald-Hall, and that as his Cousin's freind he should be happy to see me there also. To Macdonald-Hall, therefore we went, and were received with great kindness by Janetta the Daughter of Macdonald, and the Mistress of the Mansion. Janetta was then only fifteen; naturally well disposed, endowed with a susceptible Heart, and a simpathetic Disposition, she might, had these amiable qualities been properly encouraged, have been an ornament

LOVE
AND
FREINDSHIP
AND
OTHER
EARLY
WORKS

to human Nature; but unfortunately her Father possessed not a soul sufficiently exalted to admire so promising a Disposition, and had endeavoured by every means on his power to prevent it encreasing with her Years. He had actually so far extinguished the natural noble Sensibility of her Heart, as to prevail on her to accept an offer from a young Man of his Recommendation. They were to be married in a few months, and Graham, was in the House when we arrived. WE soon saw through his character. He was just such a Man as one might have expected to be the choice of Macdonald. They said he was Sensible, well-informed, and Agreable; we did not pretend to Judge of such trifles, but as we were convinced he had no soul, that he had never read the sorrows of Werter, and that his Hair bore not the least resemblance to auburn, we were certain that Janetta could feel no affection for him, or at least that she ought to feel none. The very circumstance of his being her father's choice too, was so much in his disfavour, that had he been deserving her, in every other respect yet *that* of itself ought to have been a sufficient reason in the Eyes of Janetta for rejecting him. These considerations we were determined to represent to her in their proper light and doubted not of meeting with the desired success from one naturally so well disposed; whose errors in the affair had only arisen from a want of proper confidence in her own opinion, and a suitable contempt of her father's. We found her indeed all that our warmest wishes could have hoped for; we had no difficulty to convince her that it was impossible she could love Graham, or that it was her Duty to disobey her Father; the only thing at which she rather seemed to hesitate was our assertion that she must be attached to some other Person. For some time, she persevered in declaring that she knew no other young man for whom she had the the smallest Affection; but upon explaining the impossibility of such a thing she said that she beleived she *did like* Captain M'Kenrie better than any one she knew besides. This confession satisfied us and after having enumerated the good Qualities of M'Kenrie and assured her that she was violently in love with him, we desired to know whether he had ever in any wise declared his affection to her.

"So far from having ever declared it, I have no reason to imagine that he has ever felt any for me." said Janetta. "That he certainly adores you (replied Sophia) there can be no doubt—. The Attachment must be reciprocal. Did he never

gaze on you with admiration—tenderly press your hand—
drop an involantary tear—and leave the room abruptly?"
"Never (replied she) that I remember—he has always left
the room indeed when his visit has been ended, but has
never gone away particularly abruptly or without making
a bow." Indeed my Love (said I) you must be mistaken—for it
is absolutely impossible that he should ever have left you but
with Confusion, Despair, and Precipitation. Consider but for
a moment Janetta, and you must be convinced how absurd
it is to suppose that he could ever make a Bow, or behave like
any other Person." Having settled this Point to our satisfaction,
the next we took into consideration was, to determine in what
manner we should inform M'Kenrie of the favourable Opinion
Janetta entertained of him . . . We at length agreed to acquaint
him with it by an anonymous Letter which Sophia drew up
in the following manner.

"Oh! happy Lover of the beautifull Janetta, oh! amiable
Possessor of *her* Heart whose hand is destined to another,
why do you thus delay a confession of your attachment to
the amiable Object of it? Oh! consider that a few weeks will
at once put an end to every flattering Hope that you may now
entertain, by uniting the unfortunate Victim of her father's
Cruelty to the execrable and detested Graham."

"Alas! why do you thus so cruelly connive at the projected
Misery of her and of yourself by delaying to communicate that
scheme which had doubtless long possessed your imagination? A secret Union will at once secure the felicity of both."

The amiable M'Kenrie, whose modesty as he afterwards
assured us had been the only reason of his having so long
concealed the violence of his affection for Janetta, on
receiving this Billet flew on the wings of Love to Macdonald-
Hall, and so powerfully pleaded his Attachment to her who
inspired it, that after a few more private interveiws, Sophia
and I experienced the satisfaction of seeing them depart for
Gretna-Green, which they chose for the celebration of their
Nuptials, in preference to any other place although it was
at a considerable distance from Macdonald-Hall.

Adeiu
Laura.

LOVE
AND
FREINDSHIP
AND
OTHER
EARLY
WORKS

They had been gone nearly a couple of Hours, before either Mac-donald or Graham had entertained any suspicion of the affair. And they might not even then have suspected it, but for the following little Accident. Sophia happening one day to open a private Drawer in Macdonald's Library with one of her own keys, discovered that it was the Place where he kept his Papers of consequence and amongst them some bank notes of considerable amount. This discovery she imparted to me; and having agreed together that it would be a proper treatment of so vile a Wretch as Macdonald to deprive him of money, perhaps dishonestly gained, it was determined that the next time we should either of us happen to go that way, we would take one or more of the Bank notes from the drawer. This well meant Plan we had often successfully put in Execution; but alas! on the very day of Janetta's Escape, as Sophia was majestically removing the 5th Bank-note from the Drawer to her own purse, she was suddenly most impertinently interrupted in her employment by the entrance of Macdonald himself, in a most abrupt and precipitate Manner. Sophia (who though naturally all winning sweetness could when occasions demanded it call forth the Dignity of her sex) instantly put on a most forbidding look, and darting an angry frown on the undaunted culprit, demanded in a haughty tone of voice "Wherefore her retirement was thus insolently broken in on?" The unblushing Macdonald, without even endeavouring to exculpate himself from the crime he was charged with, meanly endeavoured to reproach Sophia with ignobly defrauding him of his money . . . The dignity of Sophia was wounded; "Wretch (exclaimed she, hastily replacing the Bank-note in the Drawer) how darest thou to accuse me of an Act, of which the bare idea makes me blush?" The base wretch was still unconvinced and continued to upbraid the justly-offended Sophia in such opprobious Language, that at length he so greatly provoked the gentle sweetness of her Nature, as to induce her to revenge herself on him by informing him of Janetta's Elopement, and of the active Part we had both taken in the affair. At this period of their Quarrel I entered the Library and was as you may imagine equally offended as Sophia at the ill-grounded accusations of the malevolent and contemptible Macdonald. "Base Miscreant! (cried I) how canst thou thus undauntedly endeavour to sully the spotless reputation of such bright Excellence? Why dost thou not suspect MY innocence as soon?" "Be satisfied Madam (replied he) I *do* suspect it, and therefore must desire that you will both leave this House in less than half an hour."

"We shall go willingly; (answered Sophia) our hearts have long detested thee, and nothing but our freindship for thy Daughter could have induced us to remain so long beneath thy roof."

"Your Freindship for my Daughter has indeed been most powerfully exerted by throwing her into the arms of an unprincipled Fortune-hunter." (replied he)

"Yes, (exclaimed I) amidst every misfortune, it will afford us some consolation to reflect that by this one act of Freindship to Janetta, we have amply discharged every obligation that we have received from her father."

"It must indeed be a most gratefull reflection, to your exalted minds." (said he.)

As soon as we had packed up our wardrobe and valuables, we left Macdonald Hall, and after having walked about a mile and a half we sate down by the side of a clear limpid stream to refresh our exhausted limbs. The place was suited to meditation. A grove of full-grown Elms sheltered us from the East—. A Bed of full-grown Nettles from the West—. Before us ran the murmuring brook and behind us ran the turn-pike road. We were in a mood for contemplation and in a Disposition to enjoy so beautifull a spot. A mutual silence which had for some time reigned between us, was at length broke by my exclaiming—"What a lovely scene! Alas why are not Edward and Augustus here to enjoy its Beauties with us?"

"Ah! my beloved Laura (cried Sophia) for pity's sake forbear recalling to my remembrance the unhappy situation of my imprisoned Husband. Alas, what would I not give to learn the fate of my Augustus! to know if he is still in Newgate, or if he is yet hung. But never shall I be able so far to conquer my tender sensibility as to enquire after him. Oh! do not I beseech you ever let me again hear you repeat his beloved name—. It affects me too deeply—. I cannot bear to hear him mentioned it wounds my feelings."

LOVE
AND
FREINDSHIP
AND
OTHER
EARLY
WORKS

"Excuse me my Sophia for having thus unwillingly offended you—" replied I—and then changing the conversation, desired her to admire the noble Grandeur of the Elms which sheltered us from the Eastern Zephyr. "Alas! my Laura (returned she) avoid so melancholy a subject, I intreat you. Do not again wound my Sensibility by observations on those elms. They remind me of Augustus. He was like them, tall, magestic—he possessed that noble grandeur which you admire in them."

I was silent, fearfull lest I might any more unwillingly distress her by fixing on any other subject of conversation which might again remind her of Augustus.

"Why do you not speak my Laura? (said she after a short pause) "I cannot support this silence you must not leave me to my own reflections; they ever recur to Augustus."

"What a beautifull sky! (said I) How charmingly is the azure varied by those delicate streaks of white!"

"Oh! my Laura (replied she hastily withdrawing her Eyes from a momentary glance at the sky) do not thus distress me by calling my Attention to an object which so cruelly reminds me of my Augustus's blue sattin waistcoat striped in white! In pity to your unhappy freind avoid a subject so distressing." What could I do? The feelings of Sophia were at that time so exquisite, and the tenderness she felt for Augustus so poignant that I had not power to start any other topic, justly fearing that it might in some unforseen manner again awaken all her sensibility by directing her thoughts to her Husband. Yet to be silent would be cruel; she had intreated me to talk.

From this Dilemma I was most fortunately releived by an accident truly apropos; it was the lucky overturning of a Gentleman's Phaeton, on the road which ran murmuring behind us. It was a most fortunate accident as it diverted the attention of Sophia from the melancholy reflections which she had been before indulging. We instantly quitted our seats and ran to the rescue of those who but a few moments before had been in so elevated a situation as a fashionably high Phaeton, but who were now laid low and sprawling in the Dust. "What an ample subject for reflection on the uncertain Enjoyments of this World, would not that Phaeton and the Life of Cardinal Wolsey afford a thinking Mind!" said I to Sophia as we were hastening to the field of Action.

She had not time to answer me, for every thought was now engaged by the horrid spectacle before us. Two Gentlemen most elegantly attired but weltering in their blood was what first struck our Eyes—we approached—they were Edward and Augustus—. Yes dearest Marianne they were our Husbands.

Sophia shreiked and fainted on the ground—I screamed and instantly ran mad—. We remained thus mutually deprived of our senses, some minutes, and on regaining them were deprived of them again. For an Hour and a Quarter did we continue in this unfortunate situation—Sophia fainting every moment and I running mad as often. At length a groan from the hapless Edward (who alone retained any share of life) restored us to ourselves. Had we indeed before imagined that either of them lived, we should have been more sparing of our Greif—but as we had supposed when we first beheld them that they were no more, we knew that nothing could remain to be done but what we were about. No sooner did we therefore hear my Edward's groan than postponing our lamentations for the present, we hastily ran to the Dear Youth and kneeling on each side of him implored him not to die—. "Laura (said He fixing his now languid Eyes on me) I fear I have been overturned."

I was overjoyed to find him yet sensible.

"Oh! tell me Edward (said I) tell me I beseech you before you die, what has befallen you since that unhappy Day in which Augustus was arrested and we were separated—"

"I will" (said he) and instantly fetching a deep sigh, Expired—. Sophia immediately sank again into a swoon—. MY greif was more audible. My Voice faltered, My Eyes assumed a vacant stare, my face became as pale as Death, and my senses were considerably impaired—.

"Talk not to me of Phaetons (said I, raving in a frantic, incoherent manner)—Give me a violin—. I'll play to him and sooth him in his melancholy Hours—Beware ye gentle Nymphs of Cupid's Thunderbolts, avoid the piercing shafts of Jupiter—Look at that grove of Firs—I see a Leg of Mutton—They told me Edward was not Dead; but they deceived me—they took him for a cucumber—" Thus I continued wildly exclaiming on my Edward's Death—. For two Hours did I rave thus madly and should not then have left off, as I was not in the least fatigued, had not Sophia who was just recovered from her swoon, intreated me to consider that Night was now approaching and that the Damps began to fall. "And whither shall we go (said I) to shelter us from either?" "To that white Cottage." (replied she pointing to a neat Building which rose up amidst the grove of Elms and which I had not before observed—) I agreed and we instantly walked to it—we knocked at the door—it was opened by an old

LOVE
AND
FREINDSHIP
AND
OTHER
EARLY
WORKS

woman; on being requested to afford us a Night's Lodging, she informed us that her House was but small, that she had only two Bedrooms, but that However we should be wellcome to one of them. We were satisfied and followed the good woman into the House where we were greatly cheered by the sight of a comfortable fire—. She was a widow and had only one Daughter, who was then just seventeen—One of the best of ages; but alas! she was very plain and her name was Bridget . . . Nothing therfore could be expected from her— she could not be supposed to possess either exalted Ideas, Delicate Feelings or refined Sensibilities—. She was nothing more than a mere good-tempered, civil and obliging young woman; as such we could scarcely dislike here—she was only an Object of Contempt—.

Adeiu
Laura.

●

LETTER the 14th, LAURA in continuation

Arm yourself my amiable young Freind with all the philosophy you are Mistress of; summon up all the fortitude you possess, for alas! in the perusal of the following Pages your sensibility will be most severely tried. Ah! what were the misfortunes I had before experienced and which I have already related to you, to the one I am now going to inform you of. The Death of my Father and my Mother and my Husband though almost more than my gentle Nature could support, were trifles in comparison to the misfortune I am now proceeding to relate. The morning after our arrival at the Cottage, Sophia complained of a violent pain in her delicate limbs, accompanied with a disagreable Head-ake She attributed it to a cold caught by her continued faintings in the open air as the Dew was falling the Evening before. This I feared was but too probably the case; since how could it be otherwise accounted for that I should have escaped the same indisposition, but by supposing that the bodily Exertions I had undergone in my repeated fits of frenzy had so effectually circulated and warmed my Blood as to make me proof against the chilling Damps of Night, whereas, Sophia lying totally inactive on the ground must have been exposed to all their severity. I was most seriously alarmed by her illness which trifling as it may appear to you, a certain instinctive sensibility whispered me, would in the End be fatal to her.

Alas! my fears were but too fully justified; she grew gradually worse—and I daily became more alarmed for her. At length she was obliged to confine herself solely to the Bed allotted us by our worthy Landlady—. Her disorder turned to a galloping Consumption and in a few days carried her off. Amidst all my Lamentations for her (and violent you may suppose they were) I yet received some consolation in the reflection of my having paid every attention to her, that could be offered, in her illness. I had wept over her every Day— had bathed her sweet face with my tears and had pressed her fair Hands continually in mine—. "My beloved Laura (said she to me a few Hours before she died) take warning from my unhappy End and avoid the imprudent conduct which had occasioned it . . . Beware of fainting-fits . . . Though at the time they may be refreshing and agreable yet beleive me they will in the end, if too often repeated and at improper seasons, prove destructive to your Constitution . . . My fate will teach you this . . . I die a Martyr to my greif for the loss of Augustus . . . One fatal swoon has cost me my Life . . . Beware of swoons Dear Laura . . . A frenzy fit is not one quarter so pernicious; it is an exercise to the Body and if not too violent, is I dare say conducive to Health in its consequences—Run mad as often as you chuse; but do not faint—"

These were the last words she ever addressed to me . . . It was her dieing Advice to her afflicted Laura, who has ever most faithfully adhered to it.

After having attended my lamented freind to her Early Grave, I immediately (tho' late at night) left the detested Village in which she died, and near which had expired my Husband and Augustus. I had not walked many yards from it before I was overtaken by a stage-coach, in which I instantly took a place, determined to proceed in it to Edinburgh, where I hoped to find some kind some pitying Freind who would receive and comfort me in my afflictions.

It was so dark when I entered the Coach that I could not distinguish the Number of my Fellow-travellers; I could only perceive that they were many. Regardless however of anything concerning them, I gave myself up to my own sad Reflections. A general silence prevailed—A silence, which was by nothing interrupted but by the loud and repeated snores of one of the Party.

"What an illiterate villain must that man be! (thought I to myself) What a total want of delicate refinement must he have, who can thus shock our senses by such a brutal noise! He must I am certain be capable of every bad action! There is no crime too black for such a Character!" Thus reasoned I within myself, and doubtless such were the reflections of my fellow travellers.

At length, returning Day enabled me to behold the unprincipled Scoundrel who had so violently disturbed my feelings. It was Sir Edward the father of my Deceased Husband. By his side sate Augusta, and on the same seat with me were your Mother and Lady Dorothea. Imagine my surprise at finding myself thus seated amongst my old Acquaintance. Great as was my astonishment, it was yet increased, when on looking out of Windows, I beheld the Husband of Philippa, with Philippa by his side, on the Coachbox and when on looking behind I beheld, Philander and Gustavus in the Basket. "Oh! Heavens, (exclaimed I) is it possible that I should so unexpectedly be surrounded by my nearest Relations and Connections?" These words roused the rest of the Party, and every eye was directed to the corner in which I sat. "Oh! my Isabel (continued I throwing myself across Lady Dorothea into her arms) receive once more to your Bosom the unfortunate Laura. Alas! when we last parted in the Vale of Usk, I was happy in being united to the best of Edwards; I had then a Father and a Mother, and had never known misfortunes— But now deprived of every freind but you—"

"What! (interrupted Augusta) is my Brother dead then? Tell us I intreat you what is become of him?" "Yes, cold and insensible Nymph, (replied I) that luckless swain your Brother, is no more, and you may now glory in being the Heiress of Sir Edward's fortune."

Although I had always despised her from the Day I had overheard her conversation with my Edward, yet in civility I complied with hers and Sir Edward's intreaties that I would inform them of the whole melancholy affair. They were greatly shocked—even the obdurate Heart of Sir Edward and the insensible one of Augusta, were touched with sorrow, by the unhappy tale. At the request of your Mother I related to them every other misfortune which had befallen me since we parted. Of the imprisonment of Augustus and the absence of Edward—of our arrival in Scotland—of our unexpected Meeting with our Grand-father and our cousins—of our visit to Macdonald-Hall—of the singular service we there performed towards Janetta—of her Fathers ingratitude for it ... of his inhuman Behaviour, unaccountable suspicions, and barbarous treatment of us, in obliging us to leave the House .. . of our lamentations on the loss of Edward and Augustus and finally of the melancholy Death of my beloved Companion.

Pity and surprise were strongly depictured in your Mother's countenance, during the whole of my narration, but I am sorry to say, that to the eternal reproach of her sensibility, the latter infinitely predominated. Nay, faultless as my conduct had certainly been during the whole course of my late misfortunes and adventures, she pretended to find fault with my behaviour in many of the situations in which I had been placed. As I was sensible myself, that I had always behaved in a manner which reflected Honour on my Feelings and Refinement, I paid little attention to what she said, and desired her to satisfy my Curiosity by informing me how she came there, instead of wounding my spotless reputation with unjustifiable Reproaches. As soon as she had complied with my wishes in this particular and had given me an accurate detail of every thing that had befallen her since our separation (the particulars of which if you are not already acquainted with, your Mother will give you) I applied to Augusta for the same information respecting herself, Sir Edward and Lady Dorothea.

She told me that having a considerable taste for the Beauties of Nature, her curiosity to behold the delightful scenes it exhibited in that part of the World had been so much raised by Gilpin's Tour to the Highlands, that she had prevailed on her Father to undertake a Tour to Scotland and had persuaded Lady Dorothea to accompany them. That they had arrived at Edinburgh a few Days before and from thence had made daily Excursions into the Country around in the Stage Coach they were then in, from one of which Excursions they were at that time returning. My next enquiries were concerning Philippa and her Husband, the latter of whom I learned having spent all her fortune, had recourse for subsistence to the talent in which, he had always most excelled, namely, Driving, and that having sold every thing which belonged to them except their Coach, had converted it into a Stage and in order to be removed from any of his former Acquaintance, had driven it to Edinburgh from whence he went to Sterling every other Day. That Philippa

LOVE
AND
FREINDSHIP
AND
OTHER
EARLY
WORKS

still retaining her affection for her ungratefull Husband, had followed him to Scotland and generally accompanied him in his little Excursions to Sterling. "It has only been to throw a little money into their Pockets (continued Augusta) that my Father has always travelled in their Coach to veiw the beauties of the Country since our arrival in Scotland—for it would certainly have been much more agreable to us, to visit the Highlands in a Postchaise than merely to travel from Edinburgh to Sterling and from Sterling to Edinburgh every other Day in a crowded and uncomfortable Stage." I perfectly agreed with her in her sentiments on the affair, and secretly blamed Sir Edward for thus sacrificing his Daughter's Pleasure for the sake of a ridiculous old woman whose folly in marrying so young a man ought to be punished. His Behaviour however was entirely of a peice with his general Character; for what could be expected from a man who possessed not the smallest atom of Sensibility, who scarcely knew the meaning of simpathy, and who actually snored—.

Adeiu
Laura.

•

LETTER the 15th, LAURA in continuation.

When we arrived at the town where we were to Breakfast, I was determined to speak with Philander and Gustavus, and to that purpose as soon as I left the Carriage, I went to the Basket and tenderly enquired after their Health, expressing my fears of the uneasiness of their situation. At first they seemed rather confused at my appearance dreading no doubt that I might call them to account for the money which our Grandfather had left me and which they had unjustly deprived me of, but finding that I mentioned nothing of the Matter, they desired me to step into the Basket as we might there converse with greater ease. Accordingly I entered and whilst the rest of the party were devouring green tea and buttered toast, we feasted ourselves in a more refined and sentimental Manner by a confidential Conversation. I informed them of every thing which had befallen me during the course of my life, and at my request they related to me every incident of theirs.

"We are the sons as you already know, of the two youngest Daughters which Lord St Clair had by Laurina an italian opera girl. Our mothers could neither of them exactly ascertain who were our Father, though it is generally beleived that Philander, is the son of one Philip Jones a Bricklayer and that my Father was one Gregory Staves a Staymaker of Edinburgh. This is however of little consequence for as our Mothers were certainly never married to either of them it reflects no Dishonour on our Blood, which is of a most ancient and unpolluted kind. Bertha (the Mother of Philander) and Agatha (my own Mother) always lived together. They were neither of them very rich; their united fortunes had originally amounted to nine thousand Pounds, but as they had always lived on the principal of it, when we were fifteen it was diminished to nine Hundred. This nine Hundred they always kept in a Drawer in one of the Tables which stood in our common sitting Parlour, for the convenience of having it always at Hand. Whether it was from this circumstance, of its being easily taken, or from a wish of being independant, or from an excess of sensibility (for which we were always remarkable) I cannot now determine, but certain it is that when we had reached our 15th year, we took the nine Hundred Pounds and ran away. Having obtained this prize we were determined to manage it with eoconomy and not to spend it either with folly or Extravagance. To this purpose we therefore divided it into nine parcels, one of which we devoted to Victuals, the 2d to Drink, the 3d to Housekeeping, the 4th to Carriages, the 5th to Horses, the 6th to Servants, the 7th to Amusements, the 8th to Cloathes and the 9th to Silver Buckles. Having thus arranged our Expences for two months (for we expected to make the nine Hundred Pounds last as long) we hastened to London and had the good luck to spend it in 7 weeks and a Day which was 6 Days sooner than we had intended. As soon as we had thus happily disencumbered ourselves from the weight of so much money, we began to think of returning to our Mothers, but accidentally hearing that they were both starved to Death, we gave over the design and determined to engage ourselves to some strolling Company of Players, as we had always a turn for the Stage. Accordingly we offered our services to one and were accepted; our Company was indeed rather small, as it consisted only of the Manager his wife and ourselves, but there were fewer to pay and the only inconvenience attending it was the Scarcity of Plays which for want of People to fill the Characters, we could perform. We did not mind trifles however—. One of our most admired Performances was *Macbeth*, in which we were truly great. The Manager always played Banquo himself, his Wife my Lady Macbeth. I did the Three Witches and Philander acted all the rest. To say the truth this tragedy was not only the Best, but the only Play that we ever performed; and after having acted it all over England, and Wales, we came to Scotland to exhibit it over the remainder of Great Britain. We happened to be quartered in that very Town, where you came and met your Grandfather—. We were in the Inn-yard when his Carriage entered and perceiving by the arms to whom it belonged, and knowing that Lord St Clair was our Grandfather, we agreed to endeavour to get something from him by discovering the Relationship—. You know how well it succeeded—. Having obtained the two Hundred Pounds, we instantly left the Town, leaving our Manager and his Wife to act *Macbeth* by themselves, and took the road to Sterling, where we spent our little fortune with great *eclat*. We are now returning to Edinburgh in order to get some preferment in the Acting way; and such my Dear Cousin is our History."

I thanked the amiable Youth for his entertaining narration, and after expressing my wishes for their Welfare and Happiness, left them in their little Habitation and returned to my other Freinds who impatiently expected me.

My adventures are now drawing to a close my dearest Marianne; at least for the present.

When we arrived at Edinburgh Sir Edward told me that as the Widow of his son, he desired I would accept from his Hands of four Hundred a year. I graciously promised that I would, but could not help observing that the unsimpathetic Baronet offered it more on account of my being the Widow of Edward than in being the refined and amiable Laura.

I took up my Residence in a Romantic Village in the Highlands of Scotland where I have ever since continued, and where I can uninterrupted by unmeaning Visits, indulge in a melancholy solitude, my unceasing Lamentations for the Death of my Father, my Mother, my Husband and my Freind.

Augusta has been for several years united to Graham the Man of all others most suited to her; she became acquainted with him during her stay in Scotland.

Sir Edward in hopes of gaining an Heir to his Title and

Estate, at the same time married Lady Dorothea—. His wishes have been answered.

Philander and Gustavus, after having raised their reputation by their Performances in the Theatrical Line at Edinburgh, removed to Covent Garden, where they still exhibit under the assumed names of Luvis and Quick.

Philippa has long paid the Debt of Nature, Her Husband however still continues to drive the Stage-Coach from Edinburgh to Sterling:—

Adeiu my Dearest Marianne
Laura.

Finis
June 13th 1790.

LOVE
AND
FREINDSHIP
AND
OTHER
EARLY
WORKS

PART

II

LESLEY CASTLE

LETTER the FIRST is from Miss MARGARET LESLEY
to Miss CHARLOTTE LUTTERELL

Lesley Castle Janry 3rd—1792.

My Brother has just left us. "Matilda (said he at parting) you and Margaret will I am certain take all the care of my dear little one, that she might have received from an indulgent, and affectionate and amiable Mother." Tears rolled down his cheeks as he spoke these words—the remembrance of her, who had so wantonly disgraced the Maternal character and so openly violated the conjugal Duties, prevented his adding anything farther; he embraced his sweet Child and after saluting Matilda and Me hastily broke from us and seating himself in his Chaise, pursued the road to Aberdeen. Never was there a better young Man! Ah! how little did he deserve the misfortunes he has experienced in the Marriage state. So good a Husband to so bad a Wife! for you know my dear Charlotte that the Worthless Louisa left him, her Child and reputation a few weeks ago in company with Danvers and dishonour. Never was there a sweeter face, a finer form, or a less amiable Heart than Louisa owned! Her child already possesses the personal Charms of her unhappy Mother! May she inherit from her Father all his mental ones! Lesley is at present but five and twenty, and has already given himself up to melancholy and Despair; what a difference between him and his Father! Sir George is 57 and still remains the Beau, the flighty stripling, the gay Lad, and sprightly Youngster, that his Son was really about five years back, and that *HE* has affected to appear ever since my remembrance.

While our father is fluttering about the streets of London, gay, dissipated, and Thoughtless at the age of 57, Matilda and I continue secluded from Mankind in our old and Mouldering Castle, which is situated two miles from Perth on a bold projecting Rock, and commands an extensive veiw of the Town and its delightful Environs. But tho' retired from almost all the World, (for we visit no one but the M'Leods, The M'Kenzies, the M'Phersons, the M'Cartneys, the M'Donalds, The M'kinnons, the M'lellans, the M'kays, the Macbeths and the Macduffs) we are neither dull nor unhappy; on the contrary there never were two more lively, more agreable or more witty girls, than we are; not an hour in the Day hangs heavy on our Hands. We read, we work, we walk, and when fatigued with these Employments releive our spirits, either by a lively song, a graceful Dance, or by some smart bon-mot, and witty repartee. We are handsome my dear Charlotte, very handsome and the greatest of our Perfections is, that we are entirely insensible of them ourselves. But why do I thus dwell on myself! Let me rather repeat the praise of our dear little Neice the innocent Louisa, who is at present sweetly smiling in a gentle Nap, as she reposes on the sofa. The dear Creature is just turned of two years old; as handsome as tho' 2 and 20, as sensible as tho' 2 and 30, and as prudent as tho' 2 and 40. To convince you of this, I must inform you that she has a very fine complexion and very pretty features, that she already knows the two first letters in the Alphabet, and that she never tears her frocks—. If I have not now convinced you of her Beauty, Sense and Prudence, I have nothing more to urge in support of my assertion, and you will therefore have no way of deciding the Affair but by coming to Lesley-Castle, and by a personal acquaintance with Louisa, determine for yourself. Ah! my dear Freind, how happy should I be to see you within these venerable Walls! It is now four years since my removal from School has separated me from you; that two such tender Hearts, so closely linked together by the ties of simpathy and Freindship, should be so widely removed from each other, is vastly moving. I live in Perthshire, You in Sussex. We might meet in London, were my Father disposed to carry me there, and were your Mother to be there at the same time. We might meet at Bath, at Tunbridge, or anywhere else indeed, could we but be at the same place together. We have only to hope that such a period may arrive. My Father does not return to us till Autumn; my Brother will leave

LOVE
AND
FREINDSHIP
AND
OTHER
EARLY
WORKS

Scotland in a few Days; he is impatient to travel. Mistaken Youth! He vainly flatters himself that change of Air will heal the Wounds of a broken Heart! You will join with me I am certain my dear Charlotte, in prayers for the recovery of the unhappy Lesley's peace of Mind, which must ever be essential to that of your sincere freind M. Lesley.

•

LETTER the SECOND, From Miss C. LUTTERELL to Miss M. LESLEY in answer

Glenford Febry 12

I have a thousand excuses to beg for having so long delayed thanking you my dear Peggy for your agreable Letter, which beleive me I should not have deferred doing, had not every moment of my time during the last five weeks been so fully employed in the necessary arrangements for my sisters wedding, as to allow me no time to devote either to you or myself. And now what provokes me more than anything else is that the Match is broke off, and all my Labour thrown away. Imagine how great the Dissapointment must be to me, when you consider that after having laboured both by Night and by Day, in order to get the Wedding dinner ready by the time appointed, after having roasted Beef, Broiled Mutton, and Stewed Soup enough to last the new-married Couple through the Honey-moon, I had the mortification of finding that I had been Roasting, Broiling and Stewing both the Meat and Myself to no purpose. Indeed my dear Freind, I never remember suffering any vexation equal to what I experienced on last Monday when my sister came running to me in the store-room with her face as White as a Whipt syllabub, and told me that Hervey had been thrown from his Horse, had fractured his Scull and was pronounced by his surgeon to be in the most emminent Danger. "Good God! (said I) you dont say so? Why what in the name of Heaven will become of all the Victuals! We shall never be able to eat it while it is good. However, we'll call in the Surgeon to help us. I shall be able to manage the Sir-loin myself, my Mother will eat the soup, and You and the Doctor must finish the rest." Here I was interrupted, by seeing my poor Sister fall down to appearance Lifeless upon one of the Chests, where we keep our Table linen. I immediately called my Mother and the Maids, and at last we brought her to herself again; as soon as ever she was sensible, she expressed a determination of going instantly to Henry, and was so wildly bent on this Scheme, that we had the greatest Difficulty in the World to prevent her putting it in execution; at last however more by Force than Entreaty we prevailed on her to go into her room; we laid her upon the Bed, and she continued for some Hours in the most dreadful Convulsions. My Mother and I continued in the room with her, and when any intervals of tolerable Composure in Eloisa would allow us, we joined in heartfelt lamentations on the dreadful Waste in our provisions which this Event must occasion, and in concerting some plan for getting rid of them. We agreed that the best thing we could do was to begin eating them immediately, and accordingly we ordered up the cold Ham and Fowls, and instantly began our Devouring Plan on them with great Alacrity. We would have persuaded Eloisa to have taken a Wing of a Chicken, but she would not be persuaded. She was however much quieter than she had been; the convulsions she had before suffered having given way to an almost perfect Insensibility. We endeavoured to rouse her by every means in our power, but to no purpose. I talked to her of Henry. "Dear Eloisa (said I) there's no occasion for your crying so much about such a trifle. (for I was willing to make light of it in order to comfort her) I beg you would not mind it—You see it does not vex me in the least; though perhaps I may suffer most from it after all; for I shall not only be obliged to eat up all the Victuals I have dressed already, but must if Henry should recover (which however is not very likely) dress as much for you again; or should he die (as I suppose he will) I shall still have to prepare a Dinner for you whenever you marry any one else. So you see that tho' perhaps for the present it may afflict you to think of Henry's sufferings, Yet I dare say he'll die soon, and then his pain will be over and you will be easy, whereas my Trouble will last much longer for work as hard as I may, I am certain that the pantry cannot be cleared in less than a fortnight." Thus I did all in my power to console her, but without any effect, and at last as I saw that she did not seem to listen to me, I said no more, but leaving her with my Mother I took down the remains of The Ham and Chicken, and sent William to ask how Henry did. He was not expected to live many Hours; he died the same day. We took all possible care to break the

LOVE
AND
FREINDSHIP
AND
OTHER
EARLY
WORKS

melancholy Event to Eloisa in the tenderest manner; yet in spite of every precaution, her sufferings on hearing it were too violent for her reason, and she continued for many hours in a high Delirium. She is still extremely ill, and her Physicians are greatly afraid of her going into a Decline. We are therefore preparing for Bristol, where we mean to be in the course of the next week. And now my dear Margaret let me talk a little of your affairs; and in the first place I must inform you that it is confidently reported, your Father is going to be married; I am very unwilling to beleive so unpleasing a report, and at the same time cannot wholly discredit it. I have written to my freind Susan Fitzgerald, for information concerning it, which as she is at present in Town, she will be very able to give me. I know not who is the Lady. I think your Brother is extremely right in the resolution he has taken of travelling, as it will perhaps contribute to obliterate from his remembrance, those disagreable Events, which have lately so much afflicted him—I am happy to find that tho' secluded from all the World, neither you nor Matilda are dull or unhappy—that you may never know what it is to, be either is the wish of your sincerely affectionate C.L.

P. S. I have this instant received an answer from my freind Susan, which I enclose to you, and on which you will make your own reflections.

The enclosed LETTER

My dear CHARLOTTE You could not have applied for information concerning the report of Sir George Lesleys Marriage, to any one better able to give it you than I am. Sir George is certainly married; I was myself present at the Ceremony, which you will not be surprised at when I subscribe myself your Affectionate Susan Lesley

●

LETTER the THIRD, From Miss MARGARET LESLEY to Miss C. LUTTERELL

Lesley Castle February the 16th

I have made my own reflections on the letter you enclosed to me, my Dear Charlotte and I will now tell you what those reflections were. I reflected that if by this second Marriage Sir George should have a second family, our fortunes must be considerably diminushed—that if his Wife should be of an extravagant turn, she would encourage him to persevere in that gay and Dissipated way of Life to which little encouragement would be necessary, and which has I fear already proved but too detrimental to his health and fortune—that she would now become Mistress of those Jewels which once adorned our Mother, and which Sir George had always promised us— that if they did not come into Perthshire I should not be able to gratify my curiosity of beholding my Mother-in-law and that if they did, Matilda would no longer sit at the head of her Father's table—. These my dear Charlotte were the melancholy reflections which crowded into my imagination after perusing Susan's letter to you, and which instantly occurred to Matilda when she had perused it likewise. The same ideas, the same fears, immediately occupied her Mind, and I know not which reflection distressed her most, whether the probable Diminution of our Fortunes, or her own Consequence. We both wish very much to know whether Lady Lesley is handsome and what is your opinion of her; as you honour her with the appellation of your freind, we flatter ourselves that she must be amiable. My Brother is already in Paris. He intends to quit it in a few Days, and to begin his route to Italy. He writes in a most chearfull manner, says that the air of France has greatly recovered both his Health and Spirits; that he has now entirely ceased to think of Louisa with any degree either of Pity or Affection, that he even feels himself obliged to her for her Elopement, as he thinks it very good fun to be single again. By this, you may perceive that he has entirely regained that chearful Gaiety, and sprightly Wit, for which he was once so remarkable. When he first became acquainted with Louisa which was little more than three years ago, he was one of the most lively, the most agreable young Men of the age—. I beleive you never yet heard the particulars of his first acquaintance with her. It commenced at our cousin Colonel Drummond's; at whose house in Cumberland he spent the Christmas, in which he attained the age of two and twenty. Louisa Burton was the Daughter of a distant Relation of Mrs. Drummond, who dieing a few Months before in extreme poverty, left his only Child then about eighteen to the protection of any of his Relations who would protect her. Mrs. Drummond was the only one

LOVE
AND
FREINDSHIP
AND
OTHER
EARLY
WORKS

who found herself so disposed—Louisa was therefore removed from a miserable Cottage in Yorkshire to an elegant Mansion in Cumberland, and from every pecuniary Distress that Poverty could inflict, to every elegant Enjoyment that Money could purchase—. Louisa was naturally ill-tempered and Cunning; but she had been taught to disguise her real Disposition, under the appearance of insinuating Sweetness, by a father who but too well knew, that to be married, would be the only chance she would have of not being starved, and who flattered himself that with such an extroidinary share of personal beauty, joined to a gentleness of Manners, and an engaging address, she might stand a good chance of pleasing some young Man who might afford to marry a girl without a Shilling. Louisa perfectly entered into her father's schemes and was determined to forward them with all her care and attention. By dint of Perseverance and Application, she had at length so thoroughly disguised her natural disposition under the mask of Innocence, and Softness, as to impose upon every one who had not by a long and constant intimacy with her discovered her real Character. Such was Louisa when the hapless Lesley first beheld her at Drummond-house. His heart which (to use your favourite comparison) was as delicate as sweet and as tender as a Whipt-syllabub, could not resist her attractions. In a very few Days, he was falling in love, shortly after actually fell, and before he had known her a Month, he had married her. My Father was at first highly displeased at so hasty and imprudent a connection; but when he found that they did not mind it, he soon became perfectly reconciled to the match. The Estate near Aberdeen which my brother possesses by the bounty of his great Uncle independant of Sir George, was entirely sufficient to support him and my Sister in Elegance and Ease. For the first twelvemonth, no one could be happier than Lesley, and no one more amiable to appearance than Louisa, and so plausibly did she act and so cautiously behave that tho' Matilda and I often spent several weeks together with them, yet we neither of us had any suspicion of her real Disposition. After the birth of Louisa however, which one would have thought would have strengthened her regard for Lesley, the mask she had so long supported was by degrees thrown aside, and as probably she then thought herself secure in the affection of her Husband (which did indeed appear if possible augmented by the birth of his Child) she seemed to take no pains to prevent that affection from ever diminushing. Our visits therefore to Dunbeath, were now less frequent and by far less agreable than they used to be. Our absence was however never either mentioned or lamented by Louisa who in the society of young Danvers with whom she became acquainted at Aberdeen (he was at one of the Universities there,) felt infinitely happier than in that of Matilda and your freind, tho' there certainly never were pleasanter girls than we are. You know the sad end of all Lesleys connubial happiness; I will not repeat it—. Adeiu my dear Charlotte; although I have not yet mentioned anything of the matter, I hope you will do me the justice to beleive that I *think* and *feel*, a great deal for your Sisters affliction. I do not doubt but that the healthy air of the Bristol downs will intirely remove it, by erasing from her Mind the remembrance of Henry.

I am my dear Charlotte yrs ever M. L.

●

LETTER the FOURTH, From Miss C. LUTTERELL to Miss M. LESLEY

Bristol February 27th

My Dear Peggy I have but just received your letter, which being directed to Sussex while I was at Bristol was obliged to be forwarded to me here, and from some unaccountable Delay, has but this instant reached me—. I return you many thanks for the account it contains of Lesley's acquaintance, Love and Marriage with Louisa, which has not the less entertained me for having often been repeated to me before.

I have the satisfaction of informing you that we have every reason to imagine our pantry is by this time nearly cleared, as we left Particular orders with the servants to eat as hard as they possibly could, and to call in a couple of Chairwomen to assist them. We brought a cold Pigeon pye, a cold turkey, a cold tongue, and half a dozen Jellies with us, which we were lucky enough with the help of our Landlady, her husband, and their three children, to get rid of, in less than two days after our arrival. Poor Eloisa is still so very indifferent both in Health and Spirits, that I very much fear, the air of the Bristol

LOVE
AND
FREINDSHIP
AND
OTHER
EARLY
WORKS

downs, healthy as it is, has not been able to drive poor Henry from her remembrance.

You ask me whether your new Mother in law is handsome and amiable—I will now give you an exact description of her bodily and mental charms. She is short, and extremely well made; is naturally pale, but rouges a good deal; has fine eyes, and fine teeth, as she will take care to let you know as soon as she sees you, and is altogether very pretty. She is remarkably good-tempered when she has her own way, and very lively when she is not out of humour. She is naturally extravagant and not very affected; she never reads anything but the letters she receives from me, and never writes anything but her answers to them. She plays, sings and Dances, but has no taste for either, and excells in none, tho' she says she is passionately fond of all. Perhaps you may flatter me so far as to be surprised that one of whom I speak with so little affection should be my particular freind; but to tell you the truth, our freindship arose rather from Caprice on her side than Esteem on mine. We spent two or three days together with a Lady in Berkshire with whom we both happened to be connected—. During our visit, the Weather being remarkably bad, and our party particularly stupid, she was so good as to conceive a violent partiality for me, which very soon settled in a downright Freindship and ended in an established correspondence. She is probably by this time as tired of me, as I am of her; but as she is too Polite and I am too civil to say so, our letters are still as frequent and affectionate as ever, and our Attachment as firm and sincere as when it first commenced. As she had a great taste for the pleasures of London, and of Brighthelmstone, she will I dare say find some difficulty in prevailing on herself even to satisfy the curiosity I dare say she feels of beholding you, at the expence of quitting those favourite haunts of Dissipation, for the melancholy tho' venerable gloom of the castle you inhabit. Perhaps however if she finds her health impaired by too much amusement, she may acquire fortitude sufficient to undertake a Journey to Scotland in the hope of its Proving at least beneficial to her health, if not conducive to her happiness. Your fears I am sorry to say, concerning your father's extravagance, your own fortunes, your Mothers Jewels and your Sister's consequence, I should suppose are but too well founded. My freind herself has four thousand pounds, and will probably spend nearly as much every year in Dress and Public places, if she can get it—she will certainly not endeavour to reclaim Sir George from the manner of living to which he has been so long accustomed, and there is therefore some reason to fear that you will be very well off, if you get any fortune at all. The Jewels I should imagine too will undoubtedly be hers, and there is too much reason to think that she will preside at her Husbands table in preference to his Daughter. But as so melancholy a subject must necessarily extremely distress you, I will no longer dwell on it—.

Eloisa's indisposition has brought us to Bristol at so unfashionable a season of the year, that we have actually seen but one genteel family since we came. Mr and Mrs Marlowe are very agreable people; the ill health of their little boy occasioned their arrival here; you may imagine that being the only family with whom we can converse, we are of course on a footing of intimacy with them; we see them indeed almost every day, and dined with them yesterday. We spent a very pleasant Day, and had a very good Dinner, tho' to be sure the Veal was terribly underdone, and the Curry had no seasoning. I could not help wishing all dinner-time that I had been at the dressing it—. A brother of Mrs Marlowe, Mr Cleveland is with them at present; he is a good-looking young Man, and seems to have a good deal to say for himself. I tell Eloisa that she should set her cap at him, but she does not at all seem to relish the proposal. I should like to see the girl married and Cleveland has a very good estate. Perhaps you may wonder that I do not consider myself as well as my Sister in my matrimonial Projects; but to tell you the truth I never wish to act a more principal part at a Wedding than the superintending and directing the Dinner, and therefore while I can get any of my acquaintance to marry for me, I shall never think of doing it myself, as I very much suspect that I should not have so much time for dressing my own Wedding-dinner, as for dressing that of my freinds.

Yours sincerely
C. L.

•

LOVE
AND
FREINDSHIP
AND
OTHER
EARLY
WORKS

LETTER the FIFTH, Miss MARGARET LESLEY
to Miss CHARLOTTE LUTTERELL

Lesley Castle March 18th

On the same day that I received your last kind letter, Matilda received one from Sir George which was dated from Edinburgh, and informed us that he should do himself the pleasure of introducing Lady Lesley to us on the following evening. This as you may suppose considerably surprised us, particularly as your account of her Ladyship had given us reason to imagine there was little chance of her visiting Scotland at a time that London must be so gay. As it was our business however to be delighted at such a mark of condescension as a visit from Sir George and Lady Lesley, we prepared to return them an answer expressive of the happiness we enjoyed in expectation of such a Blessing, when luckily recollecting that as they were to reach the Castle the next Evening, it would be impossible for my father to receive it before he left Edinburgh, we contented ourselves with leaving them to suppose that we were as happy as we ought to be. At nine in the Evening on the following day, they came, accompanied by one of Lady Lesleys brothers. Her Ladyship perfectly answers the description you sent me of her, except that I do not think her so pretty as you seem to consider her. She has not a bad face, but there is something so extremely unmajestic in her little diminutive figure, as to render her in comparison with the elegant height of Matilda and Myself, an insignificant Dwarf. Her curiosity to see us (which must have been great to bring her more than four hundred miles) being now perfectly gratified, she already begins to mention their return to town, and has desired us to accompany her. We cannot refuse her request since it is seconded by the commands of our Father, and thirded by the entreaties of Mr. Fitzgerald who is certainly one of the most pleasing young Men, I ever beheld. It is not yet determined when we are to go, but when ever we do we shall certainly take our little Louisa with us.

Adeiu my dear Charlotte; Matilda unites in best wishes to you, and Eloisa, with yours ever M. L.

•

LETTER the SIXTH, LADY LESLEY
to Miss CHARLOTTE LUTTERELL

Lesley Castle March 20th

We arrived here my sweet Freind about a fortnight ago, and I already heartily repent that I ever left our charming House in Portman-square for such a dismal old weather-beaten Castle as this. You can form no idea sufficiently hideous, of its dungeon-like form. It is actually perched upon a Rock to appearance so totally inaccessible, that I expected to have been pulled up by a rope; and sincerely repented having gratified my curiosity to behold my Daughters at the expence of being obliged to enter their prison in so dangerous and ridiculous a manner. But as soon as I once found myself safely arrived in the inside of this tremendous building, I comforted myself with the hope of having my spirits revived, by the sight of two beautifull girls, such as the Miss Lesleys had been represented to me, at Edinburgh. But here again, I met with nothing but Disappointment and Surprise. Matilda and Margaret Lesley are two great, tall, out of the way, over-grown, girls, just of a proper size to inhabit a Castle almost as large in comparison as themselves. I wish my dear Charlotte that you could but behold these Scotch giants; I am sure they would frighten you out of your wits. They will do very well as foils to myself, so I have invited them to accompany me to London where I hope to be in the course of a fortnight. Besides these two fair Damsels, I found a little humoured Brat here who I beleive is some relation to them, they told me who she was, and gave me a long rigmerole story of her father and a Miss *Somebody* which I have entirely forgot. I hate scandal and detest Children. I have been plagued ever since I came here with tiresome visits from a parcel of Scotch wretches, with terrible hard-names; they were so civil, gave me so many invitations, and talked of coming again so soon, that I could not help affronting them. I suppose I shall not see them any more, and yet as a family party we are so stupid, that I do not know what to do with myself. These girls have no Music, but Scotch airs, no Drawings but Scotch Mountains, and no Books but Scotch Poems—and I hate everything Scotch. In general I can spend half the Day at my toilett with a great deal of pleasure, but why should I dress here, since there is not a creature in the House whom I have any wish to please.

LOVE
AND
FREINDSHIP
AND
OTHER
EARLY
WORKS

I have just had a conversation with my Brother in which he has greatly offended me, and which as I have nothing more entertaining to send you I will gave you the particulars of. You must know that I have for these 4 or 5 Days past strongly suspected William of entertaining a partiality to my eldest Daughter. I own indeed that had I been inclined to fall in love with any woman, I should not have made choice of Matilda Lesley for the object of my passion; for there is nothing I hate so much as a tall Woman: but however there is no accounting for some men's taste and as William is himself nearly six feet high, it is not wonderful that he should be partial to that height. Now as I have a very great affection for my Brother and should be extremely sorry to see him unhappy, which I suppose he means to be if he cannot marry Matilda, as moreover I know that his circumstances will not allow him to marry any one without a fortune, and that Matilda's is entirely dependant on her Father, who will neither have his own inclination nor my permission to give her anything at present, I thought it would be doing a good-natured action by my Brother to let him know as much, in order that he might choose for himself, whether to conquer his passion, or Love and Despair. Accordingly finding myself this Morning alone with him in one of the horrid old rooms of this Castle, I opened the cause to him in the following Manner.

"Well my dear William what do you think of these girls? for my part, I do not find them so plain as I expected: but perhaps you may think me partial to the Daughters of my Husband and perhaps you are right—They are indeed so very like Sir George that it is natural to think"—

"My Dear Susan (cried he in a tone of the greatest amazement) You do not really think they bear the least resemblance to their Father! He is so very plain!—but I beg your pardon—I had entirely forgotten to whom I was speaking—"

"Oh! pray dont mind me; (replied I) every one knows Sir George is horribly ugly, and I assure you I always thought him a fright."

"You surprise me extremely (answered William) by what you say both with respect to Sir George and his Daughters. You cannot think your Husband so deficient in personal Charms as you speak of, nor can you surely see any resemblance between him and the Miss Lesleys who are in my opinion perfectly unlike him and perfectly Handsome."

"If that is your opinion with regard to the girls it certainly is no proof of their Fathers beauty, for if they are perfectly unlike him and very handsome at the same time, it is natural to suppose that he is very plain."

"By no means, (said he) for what may be pretty in a Woman, may be very unpleasing in a Man."

"But you yourself (replied I) but a few minutes ago allowed him to be very plain."

"Men are no Judges of Beauty in their own Sex." (said he).

"Neither Men nor Women can think Sir George tolerable."

"Well, well, (said he) we will not dispute about HIS Beauty, but your opinion of his *daughters* is surely very singular, for if I understood you right, you said you did not find them so plain as you expected to do!"

"Why, do *you* find them plainer then?" (said I).

"I can scarcely beleive you to be serious (returned he) when you speak of their persons in so extroidinary a Manner. Do not you think the Miss Lesleys are two very handsome young Women?"

"Lord! No! (cried I) I think them terribly plain!"

"Plain! (replied He) My dear Susan, you cannot really think so! Why what single Feature in the face of either of them, can you possibly find fault with?"

"Oh! trust me for that; (replied I). Come I will begin with the eldest—with Matilda. Shall I, William?" (I looked as cunning as I could when I said it, in order to shame him).

"They are so much alike (said he) that I should suppose the faults of one, would be the faults of both."

"Well, then, in the first place; they are both so horribly tall!"

"They are *taller* than you are indeed." (said he with a saucy smile.)

"Nay, (said I), I know nothing of that."

"Well, but (he continued) tho' they may be above the common size, their figures are perfectly elegant; and as to their faces, their Eyes are beautifull."

"I never can think such tremendous, knock-me-down figures in the least degree elegant, and as for their eyes, they are so tall that I never could strain my neck enough to look at them."

"Nay, (replied he) I know not whether you may not be in the right in not attempting it, for perhaps they might dazzle you with their Lustre."

"Oh! Certainly." (said I, with the greatest complacency,

for I assure you my dearest Charlotte I was not in the least offended tho' by what followed, one would suppose that William was conscious of having given me just cause to be so, for coming up to me and taking my hand, he said) "You must not look so grave Susan; you will make me fear I have offended you!"

"Offended me! Dear Brother, how came such a thought in your head! (returned I) No really! I assure you that I am not in the least surprised at your being so warm an advocate for the Beauty of these girls."—

"Well, but (interrupted William) remember that we have not yet concluded our dispute concerning them. What fault do you find with their complexion?"

"They are so horridly pale."

"They have always a little colour, and after any exercise it is considerably heightened."

"Yes, but if there should ever happen to be any rain in this part of the world, they will never be able raise more than their common stock—except indeed they amuse themselves with running up and Down these horrid old galleries and Antichambers."

"Well, (replied my Brother in a tone of vexation, and glancing an impertinent look at me) if they *have* but little colour, at least, it is all their own."

This was too much my dear Charlotte, for I am certain that he had the impudence by that look, of pretending to suspect the reality of mine. But you I am sure will vindicate my character whenever you may hear it so cruelly aspersed, for you can witness how often I have protested against wearing Rouge, and how much I always told you I disliked it. And I assure you that my opinions are still the same.—. Well, not bearing to be so suspected by my Brother, I left the room immediately, and have been ever since in my own Dressing-room writing to you. What a long letter have I made of it! But you must not expect to receive such from me when I get to Town; for it is only at Lesley castle, that one has time to write even to a Charlotte Lutterell.—. I was so much vexed by William's glance, that I could not summon Patience enough, to stay and give him that advice respecting his attachment to Matilda which had first induced me from pure Love to him to begin the conversation; and I am now so thoroughly convinced by it, of his violent passion for her, that I am certain he would never hear reason on the subject, and

I shall there fore give myself no more trouble either about him or his favourite.

Adeiu my dear girl—Yrs affectionately
Susan L.

●

LETTER the SEVENTH, From Miss C. LUTTERELL
to Miss M. LESLEY

Bristol the 27th of March

I have received Letters from you and your Mother-in-law within this week which have greatly entertained me, as I find by them that you are both downright jealous of each others Beauty. It is very odd that two pretty Women tho' actually Mother and Daughter cannot be in the same House without falling out about their faces. Do be convinced that you are both perfectly handsome and say no more of the Matter. I suppose this letter must be directed to Portman Square where probably (great as is your affection for Lesley Castle) you will not be sorry to find yourself. In spite of all that people may say about Green fields and the Country I was always of opinion that London and its amusements must be very agreable for a while, and should be very happy could my Mother's income allow her to jockey us into its Public-places, during Winter. I always longed particularly to go to Vaux-hall, to see whether the cold Beef there is cut so thin as it is reported, for I have a sly suspicion that few people understand the art of cutting a slice of cold Beef so well as I do: nay it would be hard if I did not know something of the Matter, for it was a part of my Education that I took by far the most pains with. Mama always found me HER best scholar, tho' when Papa was alive Eloisa was HIS. Never to be sure were there two more different Dispositions in the World. We both loved Reading. SHE preferred Histories, and I Receipts. She loved drawing, Pictures, and I drawing Pullets. No one could sing a better song than she, and no one make a better Pye than I.—And so it has always continued since we have been no longer children. The only difference is that all disputes on the superior excellence of our Employments THEN so frequent are now no more. We have for many years entered

LOVE
AND
FREINDSHIP
AND
OTHER
EARLY
WORKS

into an agreement always to admire each other's works; I never fail listening to HER Music, and she is as constant in eating my pies. Such at least was the case till Henry Hervey made his appearance in Sussex. Before the arrival of his Aunt in our neighbourhood where she established herself you know about a twelvemonth ago, his visits to her had been at stated times, and of equal and settled Duration; but on her removal to the Hall which is within a walk from our House, they became both more frequent and longer. This as you may suppose could not be pleasing to Mrs Diana who is a professed enemy to everything which is not directed by Decorum and Formality, or which bears the least resemblance to Ease and Good-breeding. Nay so great was her aversion to her Nephews behaviour that I have often heard her give such hints of it before his face that had not Henry at such times been engaged in conversation with Eloisa, they must have caught his Attention and have very much distressed him. The alteration in my Sisters behaviour which I have before hinted at, now took place. The Agreement we had entered into of admiring each others productions she no longer seemed to regard, and tho' I constantly applauded even every Country-dance, she played, yet not even a pidgeon-pye of my making could obtain from her a single word of approbation. This was certainly enough to put any one in a Passion; however, I was as cool as a cream-cheese and having formed my plan and concerted a scheme of Revenge, I was determined to let her have her own way and not even to make her a single reproach. My scheme was to treat her as she treated me, and tho' she might even draw my own Picture or play Malbrook (which is the only tune I ever really liked) not to say so much as "Thank you Eloisa;" tho' I had for many years constantly hollowed whenever she played, Bravo, Bravissimo, Encore, Da Capo, Allegretto, Con Expressione, and Poco Presto with many other such outlandish words, all of them as Eloisa told me expressive of my Admiration; and so indeed I suppose they are, as I see some of them in every Page of every Music book, being the sentiments I imagine of the composer.

I executed my Plan with great Punctuality. I can not say success, for alas! my silence while she played seemed not in the least to displease her; on the contrary she actually said to me one day "Well Charlotte, I am very glad to find that you have at last left off that ridiculous custom of applauding my Execution on the Harpsichord till you made my head ake, and yourself hoarse. I feel very much obliged to you for keeping your admiration to yourself." I never shall forget the very witty answer I made to this speech. "Eloisa (said I) I beg you would be quite at your Ease with respect to all such fears in future, for be assured that I shall always keep my admiration to myself and my own pursuits and never extend it to yours." This was the only very severe thing I ever said in my Life; not but that I have often felt myself extremely satirical but it was the only time I ever made my feelings public.

I suppose there never were two Young people who had a greater affection for each other than Henry and Eloisa; no, the Love of your Brother for Miss Burton could not be so strong tho' it might be more violent. You may imagine therefore how provoked my Sister must have been to have him play her such a trick. Poor girl! she still laments his Death with undiminished constancy, notwithstanding he has been dead more than six weeks; but some People mind such things more than others. The ill state of Health into which his loss has thrown her makes her so weak, and so unable to support the least exertion, that she has been in tears all this Morning merely from having taken leave of Mrs. Marlowe who with her Husband, Brother and Child are to leave Bristol this morning. I am sorry to have them go because they are the only family with whom we have here any acquaintance, but I never thought of crying; to be sure Eloisa and Mrs Marlowe have always been more together than with me, and have therefore contracted a kind of affection for each other, which does not make Tears so inexcusable in them as they would be in me. The Marlowes are going to Town; Cliveland accompanies them; as neither Eloisa nor I could catch him I hope you or Matilda may have better Luck. I know not when we shall leave Bristol, Eloisa's spirits are so low that she is very averse to moving, and yet is certainly by no means mended by her residence here. A week or two will I hope determine our Measures—in the mean time believe me and etc—and etc—

Charlotte Lutterell.

●

LOVE
AND
FREINDSHIP
AND
OTHER
EARLY
WORKS

LETTER the EIGHTH, Miss LUTTERELL to Mrs MARLOWE

Bristol April 4th

I feel myself greatly obliged to you my dear Emma for such a mark of your affection as I flatter myself was conveyed in the proposal you made me of our Corresponding; I assure you that it will be a great releif to me to write to you and as long as my Health and Spirits will allow me, you will find me a very constant correspondent; I will not say an entertaining one, for you know my situation suffciently not to be ignorant that in me Mirth would be improper and I know my own Heart too well not to be sensible that it would be unnatural. You must not expect news for we see no one with whom we are in the least acquainted, or in whose proceedings we have any Interest. You must not expect scandal for by the same rule we are equally debarred either from hearing or inventing it.—You must expect from me nothing but the melancholy effusions of a broken Heart which is ever reverting to the Happiness it once enjoyed and which ill supports its present wretchedness. The Possibility of being able to write, to speak, to you of my lost Henry will be a luxury to me, and your goodness will not I know refuse to read what it will so much releive my Heart to write. I once thought that to have what is in general called a Freind (I mean one of my own sex to whom I might speak with less reserve than to any other person) independant of my sister would never be an object of my wishes, but how much was I mistaken! Charlotte is too much engrossed by two confidential correspondents of that sort, to supply the place of one to me, and I hope you will not think me girlishly romantic, when I say that to have some kind and compassionate Freind who might listen to my sorrows without endeavouring to console me was what I had for some time wished for, when our acquaintance with you, the intimacy which followed it and the particular affectionate attention you paid me almost from the first, caused me to entertain the flattering Idea of those attentions being improved on a closer acquaintance into a Freindship which, if you were what my wishes formed you would be the greatest Happiness I could be capable of enjoying. To find that such Hopes are realised is a satisfaction indeed, a satisfaction which is now almost the only one I can ever experience.—I feel myself so languid that I am sure were you with me you would oblige me to leave off writing, and I cannot give you a greater proof of my affection for you than by acting, as I know you would wish me to do, whether Absent or Present.

I am my dear Emmas sincere freind
E. L.

•

LETTER the NINTH, Mrs MARLOWE to Miss LUTTERELL

Grosvenor Street, April 10th

Need I say my dear Eloisa how wellcome your letter was to me I cannot give a greater proof of the pleasure I received from it, or of the Desire I feel that our Correspondence may be regular and frequent than by setting you so good an example as I now do in answering it before the end of the week—. But do not imagine that I claim any merit in being so punctual; on the contrary I assure you, that it is a far greater Gratification to me to write to you, than to spend the Evening either at a Concert or a Ball. Mr Marlowe is so desirous of my appearing at some of the Public places every evening that I do not like to refuse him, but at the same time so much wish to remain at Home, that independant of the Pleasure I experience in devoting any portion of my Time to my Dear Eloisa, yet the Liberty I claim from having a letter to write of spending an Evening at home with my little Boy, you know me well enough to be sensible, will of itself be a sufficient Inducement (if one is necessary) to my maintaining with Pleasure a Correspondence with you. As to the subject of your letters to me, whether grave or merry, if they concern you they must be equally interesting to me; not but that I think the melancholy Indulgence of your own sorrows by repeating them and dwelling on them to me, will only encourage and increase them, and that it will be more prudent in you to avoid so sad a subject; but yet knowing as I do what a soothing and melancholy Pleasure it must afford you, I cannot prevail on myself to deny you so great an Indulgence, and will only insist on your not expecting me to encourage you in it, by my own letters; on the contrary I intend to fill them with such lively Wit and enlivening Humour as shall even provoke a smile in the sweet but sorrowfull countenance of my Eloisa.

In the first place you are to learn that I have met your sisters three freinds Lady Lesley and her Daughters, twice in Public since I have been here. I know you will be impatient to hear my opinion of the Beauty of three Ladies of whom you have heard so much. Now, as you are too ill and too unhappy to be vain, I think I may venture to inform you that I like none of their faces so well as I do your own. Yet they are all handsome—Lady Lesley indeed I have seen before; her Daughters I beleive would in general be said to have a finer face than her Ladyship, and yet what with the charms of a Blooming complexion, a little Affectation and a great deal of small-talk, (in each of which she is superior to the young Ladies) she will I dare say gain herself as many admirers as the more regular features of Matilda, and Margaret. I am sure you will agree with me in saying that they can none of them be of a proper size for real Beauty, when you know that two of them are taller and the other shorter than ourselves. In spite of this Defect (or rather by reason of it) there is something very noble and majestic in the figures of the Miss Lesleys, and something agreably lively in the appearance of their pretty little Mother-in-law. But tho' one may be majestic and the other lively, yet the faces of neither possess that Bewitching sweetness of my Eloisas, which her present languor is so far from diminushing. What would my Husband and Brother say of us, if they knew all the fine things I have been saying to you in this letter. It is very hard that a pretty woman is never to be told she is so by any one of her own sex without that person's being suspected to be either her determined Enemy, or her professed Toad-eater. How much more amiable are women in that particular! One man may say forty civil things to another without our supposing that he is ever paid for it, and provided he does his Duty by our sex, we care not how Polite he is to his own.

Mrs Lutterell will be so good as to accept my compliments, Charlotte, my Love, and Eloisa the best wishes for the recovery of her Health and Spirits that can be offered by her affectionate Freind E. Marlowe.

I am afraid this letter will be but a poor specimen of my Powers in the witty way; and your opinion of them will not be greatly increased when I assure you that I have been as entertaining as I possibly could.

•

LETTER the TENTH, From Miss MARGARET LESLEY
to Miss CHARLOTTE LUTTERELL

Portman Square April 13th

MY DEAR CHARLOTTE We left Lesley-Castle on the 28th of last Month, and arrived safely in London after a Journey of seven Days; I had the pleasure of finding your Letter here waiting my Arrival, for which you have my grateful Thanks. Ah! my dear Freind I every day more regret the serene and tranquil Pleasures of the Castle we have left, in exchange for the uncertain and unequal Amusements of this vaunted City. Not that I will pretend to assert that these uncertain and unequal Amusements are in the least Degree unpleasing to me; on the contrary I enjoy them extremely and should enjoy them even more, were I not certain that every appearance I make in Public but rivetts the Chains of those unhappy Beings whose Passion it is impossible not to pity, tho' it is out of my power to return. In short my Dear Charlotte it is my sensibility for the sufferings of so many amiable young Men, my Dislike of the extreme admiration I meet with, and my aversion to being so celebrated both in Public, in Private, in Papers, and in Printshops, that are the reasons why I cannot more fully enjoy, the Amusements so various and pleasing of London. How often have I wished that I possessed as little Personal Beauty as you do; that my figure were as inelegant; my face as unlovely; and my appearance as unpleasing as yours! But ah! what little chance is there of so desirable an Event; I have had the small-pox, and must therefore submit to my unhappy fate.

I am now going to intrust you my dear Charlotte with a secret which has long disturbed the tranquility of my days, and which is of a kind to require the most inviolable Secrecy from you. Last Monday se'night Matilda and I accompanied Lady Lesley to a Rout at the Honourable Mrs Kickabout's; we were escorted by Mr Fitzgerald who is a very amiable young Man in the main, tho' perhaps a little singular in his Taste—He is in love with Matilda—. We had scarcely paid our Compliments to the Lady of the House and curtseyed to half a score different people when my Attention was attracted by the appearance of a Young Man the most lovely of his Sex, who at that moment entered the Room with another Gentleman and Lady. From the first moment I beheld him, I was certain that

LOVE
AND
FREINDSHIP
AND
OTHER
EARLY
WORKS

on him depended the future Happiness of my Life. Imagine my surprise when he was introduced to me by the name of Cleveland—I instantly recognised him as the Brother of Mrs Marlowe, and the acquaintance of my Charlotte at Bristol. Mr and Mrs M. were the gentleman and Lady who accompanied him. (You do not think Mrs Marlowe handsome?) The elegant address of Mr Cleveland, his polished Manners and Delightful Bow, at once confirmed my attachment. He did not speak; but I can imagine everything he would have said, had he opened his Mouth. I can picture to myself the cultivated Understanding, the Noble sentiments, and elegant Language which would have shone so conspicuous in the conversation of Mr Cleveland. The approach of Sir James Gower (one of my too numerous admirers) prevented the Discovery of any such Powers, by putting an end to a Conversation we had never commenced, and by attracting my attention to himself. But oh! how inferior are the accomplishments of Sir James to those of his so greatly envied Rival! Sir James is one of the most frequent of our Visitors, and is almost always of our Parties. We have since often met Mr and Mrs Marlowe but no Cleveland—he is always engaged some where else. Mrs Marlowe fatigues me to Death every time I see her by her tiresome Conversations about you and Eloisa. She is so stupid! I live in the hope of seeing her irrisistable Brother to night, as we are going to Lady Flambeaus, who is I know intimate with the Marlowes. Our party will be Lady Lesley, Matilda, Fitzgerald, Sir James Gower, and myself. We see little of Sir George, who is almost always at the gaming-table. Ah! my poor Fortune where art thou by this time? We see more of Lady L. who always makes her appearance (highly rouged) at Dinner-time. Alas! what Delightful Jewels will she be decked in this evening at Lady Flambeau's! Yet I wonder how she can herself delight in wearing them; surely she must be sensible of the ridiculous impropriety of loading her little diminutive figure with such superfluous ornaments; is it possible that she can not know how greatly superior an elegant simplicity is to the most studied apparel? Would she but Present them to Matilda and me, how greatly should we be obliged to her, How becoming would Diamonds be on our fine majestic figures! And how surprising it is that such an Idea should never have occurred to *her*. I am sure if I have reflected in this manner once, I have fifty times. Whenever I see Lady Lesley dressed in them such reflections immediately come across me. My own Mother's Jewels too! But I will say no more on so melancholy a subject—let me entertain you with something more pleasing—Matilda had a letter this morning from Lesley, by which we have the pleasure of finding that he is at Naples has turned Roman-Catholic, obtained one of the Pope's Bulls for annulling his 1st Marriage and has since actually married a Neapolitan Lady of great Rank and Fortune. He tells us moreover that much the same sort of affair has befallen his first wife the worthless Louisa who is likewise at Naples had turned Roman-catholic, and is soon to be married to a Neapolitan Nobleman of great and Distinguished merit. He says, that they are at present very good Freinds, have quite forgiven all past errors and intend in future to be very good Neighbours. He invites Matilda and me to pay him a visit to Italy and to bring him his little Louisa whom both her Mother, Step-mother, and himself are equally desirous of beholding. As to our accepting his invitation, it is at Present very uncertain; Lady Lesley advises us to go without loss of time; Fitzgerald offers to escort us there, but Matilda has some doubts of the Propriety of such a scheme— she owns it would be very agreable. I am certain she likes the Fellow. My Father desires us not to be in a hurry, as perhaps if we wait a few months both he and Lady Lesley will do themselves the pleasure of attending us. Lady Lesley says no, that nothing will ever tempt her to forego the Amusements of Brighthelmstone for a Journey to Italy merely to see our Brother. "No (says the disagreable Woman) I have once in my life been fool enough to travel I dont know how many hundred Miles to see two of the Family, and I found it did not answer, so Deuce take me, if ever I am so foolish again." So says her Ladyship, but Sir George still Perseveres in saying that perhaps in a month or two, they may accompany us.

Adeiu my Dear Charlotte
Yrs faithful Margaret Lesley.

LOVE
AND
FREINDSHIP
AND
OTHER
EARLY
WORKS

PART

III

LADY SUSAN

LADY SUSAN VERNON TO MR. VERNON

Langford, Dec.

MY DEAR BROTHER,—I can no longer refuse myself the pleasure of profiting by your kind invitation when we last parted of spending some weeks with you at Churchhill, and, therefore, if quite convenient to you and Mrs. Vernon to receive me at present, I shall hope within a few days to be introduced to a sister whom I have so long desired to be acquainted with. My kind friends here are most affectionately urgent with me to prolong my stay, but their hospitable and cheerful dispositions lead them too much into society for my present situation and state of mind; and I impatiently look forward to the hour when I shall be admitted into your delightful retirement.

I long to be made known to your dear little children, in whose hearts I shall be very eager to secure an interest I shall soon have need for all my fortitude, as I am on the point of separation from my own daughter. The long illness of her dear father prevented my paying her that attention which duty and affection equally dictated, and I have too much reason to fear that the governess to whose care I consigned her was unequal to the charge. I have therefore resolved on placing her at one of the best private schools in town, where I shall have an opportunity of leaving her myself in my way to you. I am determined, you see, not to be denied admittance at Churchhill. It would indeed give me most painful sensations to know that it were not in your power to receive me.

Your most obliged and affectionate sister,
S. VERNON.

•

LADY SUSAN VERNON TO MRS. JOHNSON

Langford.

You were mistaken, my dear Alicia, in supposing me fixed at this place for the rest of the winter: it grieves me to say how greatly you were mistaken, for I have seldom spent three months more agreeably than those which have just flown away. At present, nothing goes smoothly; the females of the family are united against me. You foretold how it would be when I first came to Langford, and Mainwaring is so uncommonly pleasing that I was not without apprehensions for myself. I remember saying to myself, as I drove to the house, "I like this man, pray Heaven no harm come of it!" But I was determined to be discreet, to bear in mind my being only four months a widow, and to be as quiet as possible: and I have been so, my dear creature; I have admitted no one's attentions but Mainwaring's. I have avoided all general flirtation whatever; I have distinguished no creature besides, of all the numbers resorting hither, except Sir James Martin, on whom I bestowed a little notice, in order to detach him from Miss Mainwaring; but, if the world could know my motive THERE they would honour me. I have been called an unkind mother, but it was the sacred impulse of maternal affection, it was the advantage of my daughter that led me on; and if that daughter were not the greatest simpleton on earth, I might have been rewarded for my exertions as I ought.

Sir James did make proposals to me for Frederica; but Frederica, who was born to be the torment of my life, chose to set herself so violently against the match that I thought it better to lay aside the scheme for the present. I have more than once repented that I did not marry him myself; and were he but one degree less contemptibly weak I certainly should: but I must own myself rather romantic in that respect, and that riches only will not satisfy me. The event of all this is very provoking: Sir James is gone, Maria highly incensed, and Mrs. Mainwaring insupportably jealous; so jealous, in short, and so enraged against me, that, in the fury of her temper, I should not be surprised at her appealing to her guardian, if she had the liberty of addressing him: but there your husband stands my friend; and the kindest, most amiable action of his life was his throwing her off for ever on her marriage. Keep up his resentment, therefore, I charge you. We are now in a sad state; no house was ever more altered; the whole party are at war, and Mainwaring scarcely dares speak to me. It is time for me to be gone; I have therefore determined on leaving them, and shall spend, I hope, a comfortable day with you in town within this week. If I am as little in favour with Mr. Johnson as ever, you must come to me at 10 Wigmore street; but I hope this may not be the case, for as Mr. Johnson, with all his faults, is a man to whom that great word "respectable" is always given, and I am known to be so intimate with his wife, his slighting me has an awkward look.

I take London in my way to that insupportable spot, a country village; for I am really going to Churchhill. Forgive me, my dear friend, it is my last resource. Were there another place in England open to me I would prefer it. Charles Vernon is my aversion; and I am afraid of his wife. At Churchhill, however, I must remain till I have something better in view. My young lady accompanies me to town, where I shall deposit her under the care of Miss Summers, in Wigmore street, till she becomes a little more reasonable. She will made good connections there, as the girls are all of the best families. The price is immense, and much beyond what I can ever attempt to pay.

Adieu, I will send you a line as soon as I arrive in town.

Yours ever,
S. VERNON.

●

MRS. VERNON TO LADY DE COURCY

Churchhill.

My dear Mother,—I am very sorry to tell you that it will not be in our power to keep our promise of spending our Christmas with you; and we are prevented that happiness by a circumstance which is not likely to make us any amends. Lady Susan, in a letter to her brother-in-law, has declared her intention of visiting us almost immediately; and as such a visit is in all probability merely an affair of convenience, it is impossible to conjecture its length. I was by no means prepared for such an event, nor can I now account for her ladyship's conduct;

Langford appeared so exactly the place for her in every respect, as well from the elegant and expensive style of living there, as from her particular attachment to Mr. Mainwaring, that I was very far from expecting so speedy a distinction, though I always imagined from her increasing friendship for us since her husband's death that we should, at some future period, be obliged to receive her. Mr. Vernon, I think, was a great deal too kind to her when he was in Staffordshire; her behaviour to him, independent of her general character, has been so inexcusably artful and ungenerous since our marriage was first in agitation that no one less amiable and mild than himself could have overlooked it all; and though, as his brother's widow, and in narrow circumstances, it was proper to render her pecuniary assistance, I cannot help thinking his pressing invitation to her to visit us at Churchhill perfectly unnecessary. Disposed, however, as he always is to think the best of everyone, her display of grief, and professions of regret, and general resolutions of prudence, were sufficient to soften his heart and make him really confide in her sincerity; but, as for myself, I am still unconvinced, and plausibly as her ladyship has now written, I cannot make up my mind till I better understand her real meaning in coming to us. You may guess, therefore, my dear madam, with what feelings I look forward to her arrival. She will have occasion for all those attractive powers for which she is celebrated to gain any share of my regard; and I shall certainly endeavour to guard myself against their influence, if not accompanied by something more substantial. She expresses a most eager desire of being acquainted with me, and makes very gracious mention of my children but I am not quite weak enough to suppose a woman who has behaved with inattention, if not with unkindness, to her own child, should be attached to any of mine. Miss Vernon is to be placed at a school in London before her mother comes to us which I am glad of, for her sake and my own. It must be to her advantage to be separated from her mother, and a girl of sixteen who has received so wretched an education, could not be a very desirable companion here. Reginald has long wished, I know, to see the captivating Lady Susan, and we shall depend on his joining our party soon. I am glad to hear that my father continues so well; and am, with best love, etc.,

CATHERINE VERNON.

LOVE
AND
FREINDSHIP
AND
OTHER
EARLY
WORKS

MR. DE COURCY TO MRS. VERNON

Parklands.

My dear Sister,—I congratulate you and Mr. Vernon on being about to receive into your family the most accomplished coquette in England. As a very distinguished flirt I have always been taught to consider her, but it has lately fallen in my way to hear some particulars of her conduct at Langford: which prove that she does not confine herself to that sort of honest flirtation which satisfies most people, but aspires to the more delicious gratification of making a whole family miserable. By her behaviour to Mr. Mainwaring she gave jealousy and wretchedness to his wife, and by her attentions to a young man previously attached to Mr. Mainwaring's sister deprived an amiable girl of her lover.

I learnt all this from Mr. Smith, now in this neighbourhood (I have dined with him, at Hurst and Wilford), who is just come from Langford where he was a fortnight with her ladyship, and who is therefore well qualified to make the communication.

What a woman she must be! I long to see her, and shall certainly accept your kind invitation, that I may form some idea of those bewitching powers which can do so much—engaging at the same time, and in the same house, the affections of two men, who were neither of them at liberty to bestow them—and all this without the charm of youth! I am glad to find Miss Vernon does not accompany her mother to Churchhill, as she has not even manners to recommend her; and, according to Mr. Smith's account, is equally dull and proud. Where pride and stupidity unite there can be no dissimulation worthy notice, and Miss Vernon shall be consigned to unrelenting contempt; but by all that I can gather Lady Susan possesses a degree of captivating deceit which it must be pleasing to witness and detect. I shall be with you very soon, and am ever,

Your affectionate brother,
R. DE COURCY.

•

LADY SUSAN VERNON TO MRS. JOHNSON

Churchhill.

I received your note, my dear Alicia, just before I left town, and rejoice to be assured that Mr. Johnson suspected nothing of your engagement the evening before. It is undoubtedly better to deceive him entirely, and since he will be stubborn he must be tricked. I arrived here in safety, and have no reason to complain of my reception from Mr. Vernon; but I confess myself not equally satisfied with the behaviour of his lady. She is perfectly well-bred, indeed, and has the air of a woman of fashion, but her manners are not such as can persuade me of her being prepossessed in my favour. I wanted her to be delighted at seeing me. I was as amiable as possible on the occasion, but all in vain. She does not like me. To be sure when we consider that I DID take some pains to prevent my brother-in-law's marrying her, this want of cordiality is not very surprizing, and yet it shows an illiberal and vindictive spirit to resent a project which influenced me six years ago, and which never succeeded at last.

I am sometimes disposed to repent that I did not let Charles buy Vernon Castle, when we were obliged to sell it; but it was a trying circumstance, especially as the sale took place exactly at the time of his marriage; and everybody ought to respect the delicacy of those feelings which could not endure that my husband's dignity should be lessened by his younger brother's having possession of the family estate. Could matters have been so arranged as to prevent the necessity of our leaving the castle, could we have lived with Charles and kept him single, I should have been very far from persuading my husband to dispose of it elsewhere; but Charles was on the point of marrying Miss De Courcy, and the event has justified me. Here are children in abundance, and what benefit could have accrued to me from his purchasing Vernon? My having prevented it may perhaps have given his wife an unfavourable impression, but where there is a disposition to dislike, a motive will never be wanting; and as to money matters it has not withheld him from being very useful to me. I really have a regard for him, he is so easily imposed upon! The house is a good one, the furniture fashionable,

LOVE
AND
FREINDSHIP
AND
OTHER
EARLY
WORKS

and everything announces plenty and elegance. Charles is very rich I am sure; when a man has once got his name in a banking-house he rolls in money; but they do not know what to do with it, keep very little company, and never go to London but on business. We shall be as stupid as possible. I mean to win my sister-in-law's heart through the children; I know all their names already, and am going to attach myself with the greatest sensibility to one in particular, a young Frederic, whom I take on my lap and sigh over for his dear uncle's sake.

Poor Mainwaring! I need not tell you how much I miss him, how perpetually he is in my thoughts. I found a dismal letter from him on my arrival here, full of complaints of his wife and sister, and lamentations on the cruelty of his fate. I passed off the letter as his wife's, to the Vernons, and when I write to him it must be under cover to you.

Ever yours,
S. VERNON.

●

MRS. VERNON TO MR. DE COURCY

Churchhill.

Well, my dear Reginald, I have seen this dangerous creature, and must give you some description of her, though I hope you will soon be able to form your own judgment. She is really excessively pretty; however you may choose to question the allurements of a lady no longer young, I must, for my own part, declare that I have seldom seen so lovely a woman as Lady Susan. She is delicately fair, with fine grey eyes and dark eyelashes; and from her appearance one would not suppose her more than five and twenty, though she must in fact be ten years older, I was certainly not disposed to admire her, though always hearing she was beautiful; but I cannot help feeling that she possesses an uncommon union of symmetry, brilliancy, and grace. Her address to me was so gentle, frank, and even affectionate, that, if I had not known how much she has always disliked me for marrying Mr. Vernon, and that we had never met before, I should have imagined her an attached friend. One is apt, I believe, to connect assurance of manner with coquetry, and to expect that an impudent address will naturally attend an impudent mind; at least I was myself prepared for an improper degree of confidence in Lady Susan; but her countenance is absolutely sweet, and her voice and manner winningly mild. I am sorry it is so, for what is this but deceit? Unfortunately, one knows her too well. She is clever and agreeable, has all that knowledge of the world which makes conversation easy, and talks very well, with a happy command of language, which is too often used, I believe, to make black appear white. She has already almost persuaded me of her being warmly attached to her daughter, though I have been so long convinced to the contrary. She speaks of her with so much tenderness and anxiety, lamenting so bitterly the neglect of her education, which she represents however as wholly unavoidable, that I am forced to recollect how many successive springs her ladyship spent in town, while her daughter was left in Staffordshire to the care of servants, or a governess very little better, to prevent my believing what she says.

If her manners have so great an influence on my resentful heart, you may judge how much more strongly they operate on Mr. Vernon's generous temper. I wish I could be as well satisfied as he is, that it was really her choice to leave Langford for Churchhill; and if she had not stayed there for months before she discovered that her friend's manner of living did not suit her situation or feelings, I might have believed that concern for the loss of such a husband as Mr. Vernon, to whom her own behaviour was far from unexceptionable, might for a time make her wish for retirement. But I cannot forget the length of her visit to the Mainwarings, and when I reflect on the different mode of life which she led with them from that to which she must now submit, I can only suppose that the wish of establishing her reputation by following though late the path of propriety, occasioned her removal from a family where she must in reality have been particularly happy. Your friend Mr. Smith's story, however, cannot be quite correct, as she corresponds regularly with Mrs. Mainwaring. At any rate it must be exaggerated. It is scarcely possible that two men should be so grossly deceived by her at once.

Yours, etc.,
CATHERINE VERNON

Churchhill.

My dear Alicia,—You are very good in taking notice of Frederica, and I am grateful for it as a mark of your friendship; but as I cannot have any doubt of the warmth of your affection, I am far from exacting so heavy a sacrifice. She is a stupid girl, and has nothing to recommend her. I would not, therefore, on my account, have you encumber one moment of your precious time by sending for her to Edward Street, especially as every visit is so much deducted from the grand affair of education, which I really wish to have attended to while she remains at Miss Summers's. I want her to play and sing with some portion of taste and a good deal of assurance, as she has my hand and arm and a tolerable voice. I was so much indulged in my infant years that I was never obliged to attend to anything, and consequently am without the accomplishments which are now necessary to finish a pretty woman. Not that I am an advocate for the prevailing fashion of acquiring a perfect knowledge of all languages, arts, and sciences. It is throwing time away to be mistress of French, Italian, and German: music, singing, and drawing, etc., will gain a woman some applause, but will not add one lover to her list—grace and manner, after all, are of the greatest importance. I do not mean, therefore, that Frederica's acquirements should be more than superficial, and I flatter myself that she will not remain long enough at school to understand anything thoroughly. I hope to see her the wife of Sir James within a twelvemonth. You know on what I ground my hope, and it is certainly a good foundation, for school must be very humiliating to a girl of Frederica's age. And, by-the-by, you had better not invite her any more on that account, as I wish her to find her situation as unpleasant as possible. I am sure of Sir James at any time, and could make him renew his application by a line. I shall trouble you meanwhile to prevent his forming any other attachment when he comes to town. Ask him to your house occasionally, and talk to him of Frederica, that he may not forget her. Upon the whole, I commend my own conduct in this affair extremely, and regard it as a very happy instance of circumspection and tenderness. Some mothers would have insisted on their daughter's accepting so good an offer on the first overture; but I could not reconcile it to myself to force Frederica into a marriage from which her heart revolted, and instead of adopting so harsh a measure merely propose to make it her own choice, by rendering her thoroughly uncomfortable till she does accept him—but enough of this tiresome girl. You may well wonder how I contrive to pass my time here, and for the first week it was insufferably dull. Now, however, we begin to mend, our party is enlarged by Mrs. Vernon's brother, a handsome young man, who promises me some amusement. There is something about him which rather interests me, a sort of sauciness and familiarity which I shall teach him to correct. He is lively, and seems clever, and when I have inspired him with greater respect for me than his sister's kind offices have implanted, he may be an agreeable flirt. There is exquisite pleasure in subduing an insolent spirit, in making a person predetermined to dislike acknowledge one's superiority. I have disconcerted him already by my calm reserve, and it shall be my endeavour to humble the pride of these self important De Courcys still lower, to convince Mrs. Vernon that her sisterly cautions have been bestowed in vain, and to persuade Reginald that she has scandalously belied me. This project will serve at least to amuse me, and prevent my feeling so acutely this dreadful separation from you and all whom I love.

Yours ever,
S. VERNON.

•

MRS. VERNON TO LADY DE COURCY

Churchhill.

My dear Mother,—You must not expect Reginald back again for some time. He desires me to tell you that the present open weather induces him to accept Mr. Vernon's invitation to prolong his stay in Sussex, that they may have some hunting together. He means to send for his horses immediately, and it is impossible to say when you may see him in Kent. I will not disguise my sentiments on this change from you, my dear mother, though I think you had better not communicate them to my father, whose excessive anxiety about Reginald would subject him to an alarm which might seriously affect

LOVE
AND
FREINDSHIP
AND
OTHER
EARLY
WORKS

his health and spirits. Lady Susan has certainly contrived, in the space of a fortnight, to make my brother like her. In short, I am persuaded that his continuing here beyond the time originally fixed for his return is occasioned as much by a degree of fascination towards her, as by the wish of hunting with Mr. Vernon, and of course I cannot receive that pleasure from the length of his visit which my brother's company would otherwise give me. I am, indeed, provoked at the artifice of this unprincipled woman; what stronger proof of her dangerous abilities can be given than this perversion of Reginald's judgment, which when he entered the house was so decidedly against her! In his last letter he actually gave me some particulars of her behaviour at Langford, such as he received from a gentleman who knew her perfectly well, which, if true, must raise abhorrence against her, and which Reginald himself was entirely disposed to credit. His opinion of her, I am sure, was as low as of any woman in England; and when he first came it was evident that he considered her as one entitled neither to delicacy nor respect, and that he felt she would be delighted with the attentions of any man inclined to flirt with her. Her behaviour, I confess, has been calculated to do away with such an idea; I have not detected the smallest impropriety in it—nothing of vanity, of pretension, of levity; and she is altogether so attractive that I should not wonder at his being delighted with her, had he known nothing of her previous to this personal acquaintance; but, against reason, against conviction, to be so well pleased with her, as I am sure he is, does really astonish me. His admiration was at first very strong, but no more than was natural, and I did not wonder at his being much struck by the gentleness and delicacy of her manners; but when he has mentioned her of late it has been in terms of more extraordinary praise; and yesterday he actually said that he could not be surprised at any effect produced on the heart of man by such loveliness and such abilities; and when I lamented, in reply, the badness of her disposition, he observed that whatever might have been her errors they were to be imputed to her neglected education and early marriage, and that she was altogether a wonderful woman. This tendency to excuse her conduct or to forget it, in the warmth of admiration, vexes me; and if I did not know that Reginald is too much at home at Churchhill to need an invitation for lengthening his visit, I should regret Mr. Vernon's giving him any. Lady Susan's intentions are of course those of absolute coquetry, or a desire of universal admiration; I cannot for a moment imagine that she has anything more serious in view; but it mortifies me to see a young man of Reginald's sense duped by her at all.

I am, etc.,
CATHERINE VERNON.

●

MRS. JOHNSON TO LADY S. VERNON

Edward Street.

My dearest Friend,—I congratulate you on Mr. De Courcy's arrival, and I advise you by all means to marry him; his father's estate is, we know, considerable, and I believe certainly entailed. Sir Reginald is very infirm, and not likely to stand in your way long. I hear the young man well spoken of; and though no one can really deserve you, my dearest Susan, Mr. De Courcy may be worth having. Mainwaring will storm of course, but you easily pacify him; besides, the most scrupulous point of honour could not require you to wait for HIS emancipation. I have seen Sir James; he came to town for a few days last week, and called several times in Edward Street. I talked to him about you and your daughter, and he is so far from having forgotten you, that I am sure he would marry either of you with pleasure. I gave him hopes of Frederica's relenting, and told him a great deal of her improvements. I scolded him for making love to Maria Mainwaring; he protested that he had been only in joke, and we both laughed heartily at her disappointment; and, in short, were very agreeable. He is as silly as ever.

Yours faithfully,
ALICIA.

●

LOVE
AND
FREINDSHIP
AND
OTHER
EARLY
WORKS

LADY SUSAN VERNON TO MRS. JOHNSON

Churchhill.

I am much obliged to you, my dear Friend, for your advice respecting Mr. De Courcy, which I know was given with the full conviction of its expediency, though I am not quite determined on following it. I cannot easily resolve on anything so serious as marriage; especially as I am not at present in want of money, and might perhaps, till the old gentleman's death, be very little benefited by the match. It is true that I am vain enough to believe it within my reach. I have made him sensible of my power, and can now enjoy the pleasure of triumphing over a mind prepared to dislike me, and prejudiced against all my past actions. His sister, too, is, I hope, convinced how little the ungenerous representations of anyone to the disadvantage of another will avail when opposed by the immediate influence of intellect and manner. I see plainly that she is uneasy at my progress in the good opinion of her brother, and conclude that nothing will be wanting on her part to counteract me; but having once made him doubt the justice of her opinion of me, I think I may defy her. It has been delightful to me to watch his advances towards intimacy, especially to observe his altered manner in consequence of my repressing by the cool dignity of my deportment his insolent approach to direct familiarity. My conduct has been equally guarded from the first, and I never behaved less like a coquette in the whole course of my life, though perhaps my desire of dominion was never more decided. I have subdued him entirely by sentiment and serious conversation, and made him, I may venture to say, at least half in love with me, without the semblance of the most commonplace flirtation. Mrs. Vernon's consciousness of deserving every sort of revenge that it can be in my power to inflict for her ill-offices could alone enable her to perceive that I am actuated by any design in behaviour so gentle and unpretending. Let her think and act as she chooses, however. I have never yet found that the advice of a sister could prevent a young man's being in love if he chose. We are advancing now to some kind of confidence, and in short are likely to be engaged in a sort of platonic friendship. On my side you may be sure of its never being more, for if I were not attached to another person as much as I can be to anyone, I should make a point of not bestowing my affection on a man who had dared to think so meanly of me. Reginald has a good figure and is not unworthy the praise you have heard given him, but is still greatly inferior to our friend at Langford. He is less polished, less insinuating than Mainwaring, and is comparatively deficient in the power of saying those delightful things which put one in good humour with oneself and all the world. He is quite agreeable enough, however, to afford me amusement, and to make many of those hours pass very pleasantly which would otherwise be spent in endeavouring to overcome my sister-in-law's reserve, and listening to the insipid talk of her husband. Your account of Sir James is most satisfactory, and I mean to give Miss Frederica a hint of my intentions very soon.

Yours, etc.,
S. VERNON.

•

MRS. VERNON TO LADY DE COURCY

Churchhill

I really grow quite uneasy, my dearest mother, about Reginald, from witnessing the very rapid increase of Lady Susan's influence. They are now on terms of the most particular friendship, frequently engaged in long conversations together; and she has contrived by the most artful coquetry to subdue his judgment to her own purposes. It is impossible to see the intimacy between them so very soon established without some alarm, though I can hardly suppose that Lady Susan's plans extend to marriage. I wish you could get Reginald home again on any plausible pretence; he is not at all disposed to leave us, and I have given him as many hints of my father's precarious state of health as common decency will allow me to do in my own house. Her power over him must now be boundless, as she has entirely effaced all his former ill-opinion, and persuaded him not merely to forget but to justify her conduct. Mr. Smith's account of her proceedings at Langford, where he accused her of having made Mr. Mainwaring and a young man engaged to Miss Mainwaring distractedly in love with her, which Reginald firmly believed when he came here, is now, he is persuaded, only a scandalous invention. He has told me so with

LOVE
AND
FREINDSHIP
AND
OTHER
EARLY
WORKS

a warmth of manner which spoke his regret at having believed the contrary himself. How sincerely do I grieve that she ever entered this house! I always looked forward to her coming with uneasiness; but very far was it from originating in anxiety for Reginald. I expected a most disagreeable companion for myself, but could not imagine that my brother would be in the smallest danger of being captivated by a woman with whose principles he was so well acquainted, and whose character he so heartily despised. If you can get him away it will be a good thing.

Yours, etc.,
CATHERINE VERNON.

●

SIR REGINALD DE COURCY TO HIS SON

Parklands.

I know that young men in general do not admit of any enquiry even from their nearest relations into affairs of the heart, but I hope, my dear Reginald, that you will be superior to such as allow nothing for a father's anxiety, and think themselves privileged to refuse him their confidence and slight his advice. You must be sensible that as an only son, and the representative of an ancient family, your conduct in life is most interesting to your connections; and in the very important concern of marriage especially, there is everything at stake—your own happiness, that of your parents, and the credit of your name. I do not suppose that you would deliberately form an absolute engagement of that nature without acquainting your mother and myself, or at least, without being convinced that we should approve of your choice; but I cannot help fearing that you may be drawn in, by the lady who has lately attached you, to a marriage which the whole of your family, far and near, must highly reprobate. Lady Susan's age is itself a material objection, but her want of character is one so much more serious, that the difference of even twelve years becomes in comparison of small amount. Were you not blinded by a sort of fascination, it would be ridiculous in me to repeat the instances of great misconduct on her side so very generally known.

Her neglect of her husband, her encouragement of other men, her extravagance and dissipation, were so gross and notorious that no one could be ignorant of them at the time, nor can now have forgotten them. To our family she has always been represented in softened colours by the benevolence of Mr. Charles Vernon, and yet, in spite of his generous endeavours to excuse her, we know that she did, from the most selfish motives, take all possible pains to prevent his marriage with Catherine.

My years and increasing infirmities make me very desirous of seeing you settled in the world. To the fortune of a wife, the goodness of my own will make me indifferent, but her family and character must be equally unexceptionable. When your choice is fixed so that no objection can be made to it, then I can promise you a ready and cheerful consent; but it is my duty to oppose a match which deep art only could render possible, and must in the end make wretched. It is possible her behaviour may arise only from vanity, or the wish of gaining the admiration of a man whom she must imagine to be particularly prejudiced against her; but it is more likely that she should aim at something further. She is poor, and may naturally seek an alliance which must be advantageous to herself; you know your own rights, and that it is out of my power to prevent your inheriting the family estate. My ability of distressing you during my life would be a species of revenge to which I could hardly stoop under any circumstances.

I honestly tell you my sentiments and intentions: I do not wish to work on your fears, but on your sense and affection. It would destroy every comfort of my life to know that you were married to Lady Susan Vernon; it would be the death of that honest pride with which I have hitherto considered my son; I should blush to see him, to hear of him, to think of him. I may perhaps do no good but that of relieving my own mind by this letter, but I felt it my duty to tell you that your partiality for Lady Susan is no secret to your friends, and to warn you against her. I should be glad to hear your reasons for disbelieving Mr. Smith's intelligence; you had no doubt of its authenticity a month ago. If you can give me your assurance of having no design beyond enjoying the conversation of a clever woman for a short period, and of yielding admiration only to her beauty and abilities, without being blinded by them to her faults, you will restore me to happiness; but, if you cannot do this, explain to me, at least,

LOVE
AND
FREINDSHIP
AND
OTHER
EARLY
WORKS

what has occasioned so great an alteration in your opinion of her.

I am, etc., etc,
REGINALD DE COURCY

●

LADY DE COURCY TO MRS. VERNON

Parklands.

My dear Catherine,—Unluckily I was confined to my room when your last letter came, by a cold which affected my eyes so much as to prevent my reading it myself, so I could not refuse your father when he offered to read it to me, by which means he became acquainted, to my great vexation, with all your fears about your brother. I had intended to write to Reginald myself as soon as my eyes would let me, to point out, as well as I could, the danger of an intimate acquaintance, with so artful a woman as Lady Susan, to a young man of his age, and high expectations. I meant, moreover, to have reminded him of our being quite alone now, and very much in need of him to keep up our spirits these long winter evenings. Whether it would have done any good can never be settled now, but I am excessively vexed that Sir Reginald should know anything of a matter which we foresaw would make him so uneasy. He caught all your fears the moment he had read your letter, and I am sure he has not had the business out of his head since. He wrote by the same post to Reginald a long letter full of it all, and particularly asking an explanation of what he may have heard from Lady Susan to contradict the late shocking reports. His answer came this morning, which I shall enclose to you, as I think you will like to see it. I wish it was more satisfactory; but it seems written with such a determination to think well of Lady Susan, that his assurances as to marriage, etc., do not set my heart at ease. I say all I can, however, to satisfy your father, and he is certainly less uneasy since Reginald's letter. How provoking it is, my dear Catherine, that this unwelcome guest of yours should not only prevent our meeting this Christmas, but be the occasion of so much vexation and trouble! Kiss the dear children for me.

Your affectionate mother,
C. DE COURCY.

•

MR. DE COURCYTO SIR REGINALD

Churchhill.

My dear Sir,—I have this moment received your letter, which has given me more astonishment than I ever felt before. I am to thank my sister, I suppose, for having represented me in such a light as to injure me in your opinion, and give you all this alarm. I know not why she should choose to make herself and her family uneasy by apprehending an event which no one but herself, I can affirm, would ever have thought possible. To impute such a design to Lady Susan would be taking from her every claim to that excellent understanding which her bitterest enemies have never denied her; and equally low must sink my pretensions to common sense if I am suspected of matrimonial views in my behaviour to her. Our difference of age must be an insuperable objection, and I entreat you, my dear father, to quiet your mind, and no longer harbour a suspicion which cannot be more injurious to your own peace than to our understandings. I can have no other view in remaining with Lady Susan, than to enjoy for a short time (as you have yourself expressed it) the conversation of a woman of high intellectual powers. If Mrs. Vernon would allow something to my affection for herself and her husband in the length of my visit, she would do more justice to us all; but my sister is unhappily prejudiced beyond the hope of conviction against Lady Susan. From an attachment to her husband, which in itself does honour to both, she cannot forgive the endeavours at preventing their union, which have been attributed to selfishness in Lady Susan; but in this case, as well as in many others, the world has most grossly injured that lady, by supposing the worst where the motives of her conduct have been doubtful. Lady Susan had heard something so materially to the disadvantage of my sister as to persuade her that the happiness of Mr. Vernon, to whom she was always much attached, would be wholly destroyed by the marriage. And this circumstance, while it explains the true motives of Lady Susan's conduct, and removes all the blame which has been so lavished on her, may also convince us how little the general report of anyone ought to be credited; since no character, however upright, can escape the malevolence

LOVE
AND
FREINDSHIP
AND
OTHER
EARLY
WORKS

of slander. If my sister, in the security of retirement, with as little opportunity as inclination to do evil, could not avoid censure, we must not rashly condemn those who, living in the world and surrounded with temptations, should be accused of errors which they are known to have the power of committing.

I blame myself severely for having so easily believed the slanderous tales invented by Charles Smith to the prejudice of Lady Susan, as I am now convinced how greatly they have traduced her. As to Mrs. Mainwaring's jealousy it was totally his own invention, and his account of her attaching Miss Mainwaring's lover was scarcely better founded. Sir James Martin had been drawn in by that young lady to pay her some attention; and as he is a man of fortune, it was easy to see HER views extended to marriage. It is well known that Miss M. is absolutely on the catch for a husband, and no one therefore can pity her for losing, by the superior attractions of another woman, the chance of being able to make a worthy man completely wretched. Lady Susan was far from intending such a conquest, and on finding how warmly Miss Mainwaring resented her lover's defection, determined, in spite of Mr. and Mrs. Mainwaring's most urgent entreaties, to leave the family. I have reason to imagine she did receive serious proposals from Sir James, but her removing to Langford immediately on the discovery of his attachment, must acquit her on that article with any mind of common candour. You will, I am sure, my dear Sir, feel the truth of this, and will hereby learn to do justice to the character of a very injured woman. I know that Lady Susan in coming to Churchhill was governed only by the most honourable and amiable intentions; her prudence and economy are exemplary, her regard for Mr. Vernon equal even to HIS deserts; and her wish of obtaining my sister's good opinion merits a better return than it has received. As a mother she is unexceptionable; her solid affection for her child is shown by placing her in hands where her education will be properly attended to; but because she has not the blind and weak partiality of most mothers, she is accused of wanting maternal tenderness. Every person of sense, however, will know how to value and commend her well-directed affection, and will join me in wishing that Frederica Vernon may prove more worthy than she has yet done of her mother's tender care. I have now, my dear father, written my real sentiments of Lady Susan; you will know from this letter how highly I admire her abilities, and esteem her character;

but if you are not equally convinced by my full and solemn assurance that your fears have been most idly created, you will deeply mortify and distress me.

I am, etc., etc.,
R. DE COURCY.

●

MRS. VERNON TO LADY DE COURCY

Churchhill

My dear Mother,—I return you Reginald's letter, and rejoice with all my heart that my father is made easy by it: tell him so, with my congratulations; but, between ourselves, I must own it has only convinced ME of my brother's having no *present* intention of marrying Lady Susan, not that he is in no danger of doing so three months hence. He gives a very plausible account of her behaviour at Langford; I wish it may be true, but his intelligence must come from herself, and I am less disposed to believe it than to lament the degree of intimacy subsisting between them, implied by the discussion of such a subject. I am sorry to have incurred his displeasure, but can expect nothing better while he is so very eager in Lady Susan's justification. He is very severe against me indeed, and yet I hope I have not been hasty in my judgment of her. Poor woman! though I have reasons enough for my dislike, I cannot help pitying her at present, as she is in real distress, and with too much cause. She had this morning a letter from the lady with whom she has placed her daughter, to request that Miss Vernon might be immediately removed, as she had been detected in an attempt to run away. Why, or whither she intended to go, does not appear; but, as her situation seems to have been unexceptionable, it is a sad thing, and of course highly distressing to Lady Susan. Frederica must be as much as sixteen, and ought to know better; but from what her mother insinuates, I am afraid she is a perverse girl. She has been sadly neglected, however, and her mother ought to remember it. Mr. Vernon set off for London as soon as she had determined what should be done. He is, if possible, to prevail on Miss Summers to let Frederica continue with her; and if he cannot succeed, to bring her to Churchhill for the present, till some other situation can be found for her. Her ladyship is comforting herself meanwhile by strolling along the shrubbery with Reginald, calling forth all his tender feelings, I suppose, on this distressing occasion. She has been talking a great deal about it to me. She talks vastly well; I am afraid of being ungenerous, or I should say, *too* well to feel so very deeply; but I will not look for her faults; she may be Reginald's wife! Heaven forbid it! but why should I be quicker-sighted than anyone else? Mr. Vernon declares that he never saw deeper distress than hers, on the receipt of the letter; and is his judgment inferior to mine? She was very unwilling that Frederica should be allowed to come to Churchhill, and justly enough, as it seems a sort of reward to behaviour deserving very differently; but it was impossible to take her anywhere else, and she is not to remain here long. "It will be absolutely necessary," said she, "as you, my dear sister, must be sensible, to treat my daughter with some severity while she is here; a most painful necessity, but I will *endeavour* to submit to it. I am afraid I have often been too indulgent, but my poor Frederica's temper could never bear opposition well: you must support and encourage me; you must urge the necessity of reproof if you see me too lenient." All this sounds very reasonable. Reginald is so incensed against the poor silly girl. Surely it is not to Lady Susan's credit that he should be so bitter against her daughter; his idea of her must be drawn from the mother's description. Well, whatever may be his fate, we have the comfort of knowing that we have done our utmost to save him. We must commit the event to a higher power.

Yours ever, etc.,
CATHERINE VERNON.

●

LADY SUSAN TO MRS. JOHNSON

Churchhill.

Never, my dearest Alicia, was I so provoked in my life as by a letter this morning from Miss Summers. That horrid girl of mine has been trying to run away. I had not a notion of her being such a little devil before, she seemed to have all the Vernon milkiness; but on receiving the letter in which I declared my intention about Sir James, she actually attempted to elope; at least, I cannot otherwise account for her doing it. She meant, I suppose, to go to the Clarkes in Staffordshire, for she has no other acquaintances. But she shall be punished, she shall have him. I have sent Charles to town to make matters up if he can, for I do not by any means want her here. If Miss Summers will not keep her, you must find me out another school, unless we can get her married immediately. Miss S. writes word that she could not get the young lady to assign any cause for her extraordinary conduct, which confirms me in my own previous explanation of it. Frederica is too shy, I think, and too much in awe of me to tell tales, but if the mildness of her uncle should get anything out of her, I am not afraid. I trust I shall be able to make my story as good as hers. If I am vain of anything, it is of my eloquence. Consideration and esteem as surely follow command of language as admiration waits on beauty, and here I have opportunity enough for the exercise of my talent, as the chief of my time is spent in conversation.

Reginald is never easy unless we are by ourselves, and when the weather is tolerable, we pace the shrubbery for hours together. I like him on the whole very well; he is clever and has a good deal to say, but he is sometimes impertinent and troublesome. There is a sort of ridiculous delicacy about him which requires the fullest explanation of whatever he may have heard to my disadvantage, and is never satisfied till he thinks he has ascertained the beginning and end of everything. This is one sort of love, but I confess it does not particularly recommend itself to me. I infinitely prefer the tender and liberal spirit of Mainwaring, which, impressed with the deepest conviction of my merit, is satisfied that whatever I do must be right; and look with a degree of contempt on the inquisitive and doubtful fancies of that heart which seems always debating on the reasonableness of its emotions. Mainwaring is indeed, beyond all compare, superior to Reginald—superior in everything but the power of being with me! Poor fellow! he is much distracted by jealousy, which I am not sorry for, as I know no better support of love. He has been teazing me to allow of his coming into this country, and lodging somewhere near INCOG.; but I forbade everything of the kind. Those women are inexcusable who forget what is due to themselves, and the opinion of the world.

LOVE
AND
FREINDSHIP
AND
OTHER
EARLY
WORKS

Yours ever, S. VERNON.

MRS. VERNON TO LADY DE COURCY

Churchhill.

My dear Mother,—Mr. Vernon returned on Thursday night, bringing his niece with him. Lady Susan had received a line from him by that day's post, informing her that Miss Summers had absolutely refused to allow of Miss Vernon's continuance in her academy; we were therefore prepared for her arrival, and expected them impatiently the whole evening. They came while we were at tea, and I never saw any creature look so frightened as Frederica when she entered the room. Lady Susan, who had been shedding tears before, and showing great agitation at the idea of the meeting, received her with perfect self-command, and without betraying the least tenderness of spirit. She hardly spoke to her, and on Frederica's bursting into tears as soon as we were seated, took her out of the room, and did not return for some time. When she did, her eyes looked very red and she was as much agitated as before. We saw no more of her daughter. Poor Reginald was beyond measure concerned to see his fair friend in such distress, and watched her with so much tender solicitude, that I, who occasionally caught her observing his countenance with exultation, was quite out of patience. This pathetic representation lasted the whole evening, and so ostentatious and artful a display has entirely convinced me that she did in fact feel nothing. I am more angry with her than ever since I have seen her daughter; the poor girl looks so unhappy that my heart aches for her. Lady Susan is surely too severe, for Frederica does not seem to have the sort of temper to make severity necessary. She looks perfectly timid, dejected, and penitent. She is very pretty, though not so handsome as her mother, nor at all like her. Her complexion is delicate, but neither so fair nor so blooming as Lady Susan's, and she has quite the Vernon cast of countenance, the oval face and mild dark eyes, and there is peculiar sweetness in her look when she speaks either to her uncle or me, for as we behave kindly to her we have of course engaged her gratitude.

Her mother has insinuated that her temper is intractable, but I never saw a face less indicative of any evil disposition than hers; and from what I can see of the behaviour of each to the other, the invariable severity of Lady Susan and the silent dejection of Frederica, I am led to believe as heretofore that the former has no real love for her daughter, and has never done her justice or treated her affectionately. I have not been able to have any conversation with my niece; she is shy, and I think I can see that some pains are taken to prevent her being much with me. Nothing satisfactory transpires as to her reason for running away. Her kind-hearted uncle, you may be sure, was too fearful of distressing her to ask many questions as they travelled. I wish it had been possible for me to fetch her instead of him. I think I should have discovered the truth in the course of a thirty-mile journey. The small pianoforte has been removed within these few days, at Lady Susan's request, into her dressing-room, and Frederica spends great part of the day there, practising as it is called; but I seldom hear any noise when I pass that way; what she does with herself there I do not know. There are plenty of books, but it is not every girl who has been running wild the first fifteen years of her life, that can or will read. Poor creature! the prospect from her window is not very instructive, for that room overlooks the lawn, you know, with the shrubbery on one side, where she may see her mother walking for an hour together in earnest conversation with Reginald. A girl of Frederica's age must be childish indeed, if such things do not strike her. Is it not inexcusable to give such an example to a daughter? Yet Reginald still thinks Lady Susan the best of mothers, and still condemns Frederica as a worthless girl! He is convinced that her attempt to run away proceeded from no, justifiable cause, and had no provocation. I am sure I cannot say that it *had*, but while Miss Summers declares that Miss Vernon showed no signs of obstinacy or perverseness during her whole stay in Wigmore Street, till she was detected in this scheme, I cannot so readily credit what Lady Susan has made him, and wants to make me believe, that it was merely an impatience of restraint and a desire of escaping from the tuition of masters which brought on the plan of an elopement. O Reginald, how is your judgment enslaved! He scarcely dares even allow her to be handsome, and when I speak of her beauty, replies only that her eyes have no brilliancy! Sometimes he is sure she is deficient in understanding, and at others that her temper only is in fault. In short, when a person is always to deceive, it is impossible to be consistent. Lady Susan finds it necessary that Frederica should be to

LOVE
AND
FREINDSHIP
AND
OTHER
EARLY
WORKS

blame, and probably has sometimes judged it expedient to excuse her of ill-nature and sometimes to lament her want of sense. Reginald is only repeating after her ladyship.

I remain, etc., etc.,
CATHERINE VERNON.

●

FROM THE SAME TO THE SAME

Churchhill.

My dear Mother,—I am very glad to find that my description of Frederica Vernon has interested you, for I do believe her truly deserving of your regard; and when I have communicated a notion which has recently struck me, your kind impressions in her favour will, I am sure, be heightened. I cannot help fancying that she is growing partial to my brother. I so very often see her eyes fixed on his face with a remarkable expression of pensive admiration. He is certainly very handsome; and yet more, there is an openness in his manner that must be highly prepossessing, and I am sure she feels it so. Thoughtful and pensive in general, her countenance always brightens into a smile when Reginald says anything amusing; and, let the subject be ever so serious that he may be conversing on, I am much mistaken if a syllable of his uttering escapes her. I want to make him sensible of all this, for we know the power of gratitude on such a heart as his; and could Frederica's artless affection detach him from her mother, we might bless the day which brought her to Churchhill. I think, my dear mother, you would not disapprove of her as a daughter. She is extremely young, to be sure, has had a wretched education, and a dreadful example of levity in her mother; but yet I can pronounce her disposition to be excellent, and her natural abilities very good. Though totally without accomplishments, she is by no means so ignorant as one might expect to find her, being fond of books and spending the chief of her time in reading. Her mother leaves her more to herself than she did, and I have her with me as much as possible, and have taken great pains to overcome her timidity. We are very good friends, and though she never opens her lips before her mother, she talks enough when alone with me to make it clear that, if properly treated by Lady Susan, she would always appear to much greater advantage. There cannot be a more gentle, affectionate heart; or more obliging manners, when acting without restraint; and her little cousins are all very fond of her.

Your affectionate daughter,
C. VERNON

●

LADY SUSAN TO MRS. JOHNSON

Churchhill.

You will be eager, I know, to hear something further of Frederica, and perhaps may think me negligent for not writing before. She arrived with her uncle last Thursday fortnight, when, of course, I lost no time in demanding the cause of her behaviour; and soon found myself to have been perfectly right in attributing it to my own letter. The prospect of it frightened her so thoroughly, that, with a mixture of true girlish perverseness and folly, she resolved on getting out of the house and proceeding directly by the stage to her friends, the Clarkes; and had really got as far as the length of two streets in her journey when she was fortunately missed, pursued, and overtaken. Such was the first distinguished exploit of Miss Frederica Vernon; and, if we consider that it was achieved at the tender age of sixteen, we shall have room for the most flattering prognostics of her future renown. I am excessively provoked, however, at the parade of propriety which prevented Miss Summers from keeping the girl; and it seems so extraordinary a piece of nicety, considering my daughter's family connections, that I can only suppose the lady to be governed by the fear of never getting her money. Be that as it may, however, Frederica is returned on my hands; and, having nothing else to employ her, is busy in pursuing the plan of romance begun at Langford. She is actually falling in love with Reginald De Courcy! To disobey her mother by refusing an unexceptionable offer is not enough; her affections must also be given without her mother's approbation. I never saw a girl of her age bid fairer to be the sport of mankind. Her feelings are tolerably acute, and she is so charmingly artless in their display as to afford the most reasonable hope of her being ridiculous, and despised by every man who sees her.

Artlessness will never do in love matters; and that girl is born a simpleton who has it either by nature or affectation. I am not yet certain that Reginald sees what she is about, nor is it of much consequence. She is now an object of indifference to him, and she would be one of contempt were he to understand her emotions. Her beauty is much admired by the Vernons, but it has no effect on him. She is in high favour with her aunt altogether, because she is so little like myself, of course. She is exactly the companion for Mrs. Vernon, who dearly loves to be firm, and to have all the sense and all the wit of the conversation to herself: Frederica will never eclipse her. When she first came I was at some pains to prevent her seeing much of her aunt; but I have relaxed, as I believe I may depend on her observing the rules I have laid down for their discourse. But do not imagine that with all this lenity I have for a moment given up my plan of her marriage. No; I am unalterably fixed on this point, though I have not yet quite decided on the manner of bringing it about. I should not chuse to have the business brought on here, and canvassed by the wise heads of Mr. and Mrs. Vernon; and I cannot just now afford to go to town. Miss Frederica must therefore wait a little.

Yours ever,
S. VERNON.

●

MRS. VERNON TO LADY DE COURCY

Churchhill

We have a very unexpected guest with us at present, my dear Mother: he arrived yesterday. I heard a carriage at the door, as I was sitting with my children while they dined; and supposing I should be wanted, left the nursery soon afterwards, and was half-way downstairs, when Frederica, as pale as ashes, came running up, and rushed by me into her own room. I instantly followed, and asked her what was the matter. "Oh!" said she, "he is come—Sir James is come, and what shall I do?" This was no explanation; I begged her to tell me what she meant. At that moment we were interrupted by a knock at the door: it was Reginald, who came, by Lady Susan's direction, to call Frederica down. "It is Mr. De Courcy!" said she, colouring violently. "Mamma has sent for me; I must go." We all three went down together; and I saw my brother examining the terrified face of Frederica with surprise. In the breakfast-room we found Lady Susan, and a young man of gentlemanlike appearance, whom she introduced by the name of Sir James Martin—the very person, as you may remember, whom it was said she had been at pains to detach from Miss Mainwaring; but the conquest, it seems, was not designed for herself, or she has since transferred it to her daughter; for Sir James is now desperately in love with Frederica, and with full encouragement from mamma. The poor girl, however, I am sure, dislikes him; and though his person and address are very well, he appears, both to Mr. Vernon and me, a very weak young man. Frederica looked so shy, so confused, when we entered the room, that I felt for her exceedingly. Lady Susan behaved with great attention to her visitor; and yet I thought I could perceive that she had no particular pleasure in seeing him. Sir James talked a great deal, and made many civil excuses to me for the liberty he had taken in coming to Churchhill—mixing more frequent laughter with his discourse than the subject required—said many things over and over again, and told Lady Susan three times that he had seen Mrs. Johnson a few evenings before. He now and then addressed Frederica, but more frequently her mother. The poor girl sat all this time without opening her lips—her eyes cast down, and her colour varying every instant; while Reginald observed all that passed in perfect silence. At length Lady Susan, weary, I believe, of her situation, proposed walking; and we left the two gentlemen together, to put on our pelisses. As we went upstairs Lady Susan begged permission to attend me for a few moments in my dressing-room, as she was anxious to speak with me in private. I led her thither accordingly, and as soon as the door was closed, she said: "I was never more surprized in my life than by Sir James's arrival, and the suddenness of it requires some apology to you, my dear sister; though to *me*, as a mother, it is highly flattering. He is so extremely attached to my daughter that he could not exist longer without seeing her. Sir James is a young

LOVE
AND
FREINDSHIP
AND
OTHER
EARLY
WORKS

man of an amiable disposition and excellent character; a little too much of the rattle, perhaps, but a year or two will rectify *that*: and he is in other respects so very eligible a match for Frederica, that I have always observed his attachment with the greatest pleasure; and am persuaded that you and my brother will give the alliance your hearty approbation. I have never before mentioned the likelihood of its taking place to anyone, because I thought that whilst Frederica continued at school it had better not be known to exist; but now, as I am convinced that Frederica is too old ever to submit to school confinement, and have, therefore, begun to consider her union with Sir James as not very distant, I had intended within a few days to acquaint yourself and Mr. Vernon with the whole business. I am sure, my dear sister, you will excuse my remaining silent so long, and agree with me that such circumstances, while they continue from any cause in suspense, cannot be too cautiously concealed. When you have the happiness of bestowing your sweet little Catherine, some years hence, on a man who in connection and character is alike unexceptionable, you will know what I feel now; though, thank Heaven, you cannot have all my reasons for rejoicing in such an event. Catherine will be amply provided for, and not, like my Frederica, indebted to a fortunate establishment for the comforts of life." She concluded by demanding my congratulations. I gave them somewhat awkwardly, I believe; for, in fact, the sudden disclosure of so important a matter took from me the power of speaking with any clearness. She thanked me, however, most affectionately, for my kind concern in the welfare of herself and daughter; and then said: "I am not apt to deal in professions, my dear Mrs. Vernon, and I never had the convenient talent of affecting sensations foreign to my heart; and therefore I trust you will believe me when I declare, that much as I had heard in your praise before I knew you, I had no idea that I should ever love you as I now do; and I must further say that your friendship towards me is more particularly gratifying because I have reason to believe that some attempts were made to prejudice you against me. I only wish that they, whoever they are, to whom I am indebted for such kind intentions, could see the terms on which we now are together, and understand the real affection we feel for each other; but I will not detain you any longer. God bless you, for your goodness to me and my girl, and continue to you all your present happiness." What can one say of such a woman, my dear mother? Such earnestness such solemnity of expression! and yet I cannot help suspecting the truth of everything she says. As for Reginald, I believe he does not know what to make of the matter. When Sir James came, he appeared all astonishment and perplexity; the folly of the young man and the confusion of Frederica entirely engrossed him; and though a little private discourse with Lady Susan has since had its effect, he is still hurt, I am sure, at her allowing of such a man's attentions to her daughter. Sir James invited himself with great composure to remain here a few days—hoped we would not think it odd, was aware of its being very impertinent, but he took the liberty of a relation; and concluded by wishing, with a laugh, that he might be really one very soon. Even Lady Susan seemed a little disconcerted by this forwardness; in her heart I am persuaded she sincerely wished him gone. But something must be done for this poor girl, if her feelings are such as both I and her uncle believe them to be. She must not be sacrificed to policy or ambition, and she must not be left to suffer from the dread of it. The girl whose heart can distinguish Reginald De Courcy, deserves, however he may slight her, a better fate than to be Sir James Martin's wife. As soon as I can get her alone, I will discover the real truth; but she seems to wish to avoid me. I hope this does not proceed from anything wrong, and that I shall not find out I have thought too well of her. Her behaviour to Sir James certainly speaks the greatest consciousness and embarrassment, but I see nothing in it more like encouragement. Adieu, my dear mother.

Yours, etc.,
C. VERNON.

•

MISS VERNON TO MR DE COURCY

Sir,—

I hope you will excuse this liberty; I am forced upon it by the greatest distress, or I should be ashamed to trouble you. I am very miserable about Sir James Martin, and have no other way in the world of helping myself but by writing to you, for I am forbidden even speaking to my uncle and aunt on the subject;

LOVE
AND
FREINDSHIP
AND
OTHER
EARLY
WORKS

and this being the case, I am afraid my applying to you will appear no better than equivocation, and as if I attended to the letter and not the spirit of mamma's commands. But if you do not take my part and persuade her to break it off, I shall be half distracted, for I cannot bear him. No human being but *you* could have any chance of prevailing with her. If you will, therefore, have the unspeakably great kindness of taking my part with her, and persuading her to send Sir James away, I shall be more obliged to you than it is possible for me to express. I always disliked him from the first: it is not a sudden fancy, I assure you, sir; I always thought him silly and impertinent and disagreeable, and now he is grown worse than ever. I would rather work for my bread than marry him. I do not know how to apologize enough for this letter; I know it is taking so great a liberty. I am aware how dreadfully angry it will make mamma, but I remember the risk.

I am, Sir, your most humble servant,
F. S. V.

●

LADY SUSAN TO MRS. JOHNSON

Churchhill.

This is insufferable! My dearest friend, I was never so enraged before, and must relieve myself by writing to you, who I know will enter into all my feelings. Who should come on Tuesday but Sir James Martin! Guess my astonishment, and vexation—for, as you well know, I never wished him to be seen at Churchhill. What a pity that you should not have known his intentions! Not content with coming, he actually invited himself to remain here a few days. I could have poisoned him! I made the best of it, however, and told my story with great success to Mrs. Vernon, who, whatever might be her real sentiments, said nothing in opposition to mine. I made a point also of Frederica's behaving civilly to Sir James, and gave her to understand that I was absolutely determined on her marrying him. She said something of her misery, but that was all. I have for some time been more particularly resolved on the match from seeing the rapid increase of her affection for Reginald, and from not feeling secure that a knowledge of such affection might not in the end awaken a return. Contemptible as a regard founded only on compassion must make them both in my eyes, I felt by no means assured that such might not be the consequence. It is true that Reginald had not in any degree grown cool towards me; but yet he has lately mentioned Frederica spontaneously and unnecessarily, and once said something in praise of her person. HE was all astonishment at the appearance of my visitor, and at first observed Sir James with an attention which I was pleased to see not unmixed with jealousy; but unluckily it was impossible for me really to torment him, as Sir James, though extremely gallant to me, very soon made the whole party understand that his heart was devoted to my daughter. I had no great difficulty in convincing De Courcy, when we were alone, that I was perfectly justified, all things considered, in desiring the match; and the whole business seemed most comfortably arranged. They could none of them help perceiving that Sir James was no Solomon; but I had positively forbidden Frederica complaining to Charles Vernon or his wife, and they had therefore no pretence for interference; though my impertinent sister, I believe, wanted only opportunity for doing so. Everything, however, was going on calmly and quietly; and, though I counted the hours of Sir James's stay, my mind was entirely satisfied with the posture of affairs. Guess, then, what I must feel at the sudden disturbance of all my schemes; and that, too, from a quarter where I had least reason to expect it. Reginald came this morning into my dressing-room with a very unusual solemnity of countenance, and after some preface informed me in so many words that he wished to reason with me on the impropriety and unkindness of allowing Sir James Martin to address my daughter contrary to her inclinations. I was all amazement. When I found that he was not to be laughed out of his design, I calmly begged an explanation, and desired to know by what he was impelled, and by whom commissioned, to reprimand me. He then told me, mixing in his speech a few insolent compliments and ill-timed expressions of tenderness, to which I listened with perfect indifference, that my daughter had acquainted him with some circumstances concerning herself, Sir James, and me which had given him great uneasiness. In short, I found that she had in the first place actually written to him to request his interference, and that, on receiving her letter, he had conversed with her

LOVE
AND
FREINDSHIP
AND
OTHER
EARLY
WORKS

on the subject of it, in order to understand the particulars, and to assure himself of her real wishes. I have not a doubt but that the girl took this opportunity of making downright love to him. I am convinced of it by the manner in which he spoke of her. Much good may such love do him! I shall ever despise the man who can be gratified by the passion which he never wished to inspire, nor solicited the avowal of. I shall always detest them both. He can have no true regard for me, or he would not have listened to her; and *she*, with her little rebellious heart and indelicate feelings, to throw herself into the protection of a young man with whom she has scarcely ever exchanged two words before! I am equally confounded at *her* impudence and *his* credulity. How dared he believe what she told him in my disfavour! Ought he not to have felt assured that I must have unanswerable motives for all that I had done? Where was his reliance on my sense and goodness then? Where the resentment which true love would have dictated against the person defaming me—that person, too, a chit, a child, without talent or education, whom he had been always taught to despise? I was calm for some time; but the greatest degree of forbearance may be overcome, and I hope I was afterwards sufficiently keen. He endeavoured, long endeavoured, to soften my resentment; but that woman is a fool indeed who, while insulted by accusation, can be worked on by compliments. At length he left me, as deeply provoked as myself; and he showed his anger more. I was quite cool, but he gave way to the most violent indignation; I may therefore expect it will the sooner subside, and perhaps his may be vanished for ever, while mine will be found still fresh and implacable. He is now shut up in his apartment, whither I heard him go on leaving mine. How unpleasant, one would think, must be his reflections! but some people's feelings are incomprehensible. I have not yet tranquillised myself enough to see Frederica. SHE shall not soon forget the occurrences of this day; she shall find that she has poured forth her tender tale of love in vain, and exposed herself for ever to the contempt of the whole world, and the severest resentment of her injured mother.

Your affectionate
S. VERNON.

•

MRS. VERNON TO LADY DE COURCY

Churchhill.

Let me congratulate you, my dearest Mother! The affair which has given us so much anxiety is drawing to a happy conclusion. Our prospect is most delightful, and since matters have now taken so favourable a turn, I am quite sorry that I ever imparted my apprehensions to you; for the pleasure of learning that the danger is over is perhaps dearly purchased by all that you have previously suffered. I am so much agitated by delight that I can scarcely hold a pen; but am determined to send you a few short lines by James, that you may have some explanation of what must so greatly astonish you, as that Reginald should be returning to Parklands. I was sitting about half an hour ago with Sir James in the breakfast parlour, when my brother called me out of the room. I instantly saw that something was the matter; his complexion was raised, and he spoke with great emotion; you know his eager manner, my dear mother, when his mind is interested. "Catherine," said he, "I am going home to-day; I am sorry to leave you, but I must go: it is a great while since I have seen my father and mother. I am going to send James forward with my hunters immediately; if you have any letter, therefore, he can take it. I shall not be at home myself till Wednesday or Thursday, as I shall go through London, where I have business; but before I leave you," he continued, speaking in a lower tone, and with still greater energy, "I must warn you of one thing—do not let Frederica Vernon be made unhappy by that Martin. He wants to marry her; her mother promotes the match, but she cannot endure the idea of it. Be assured that I speak from the fullest conviction of the truth of what I say; I know that Frederica is made wretched by Sir James's continuing here. She is a sweet girl, and deserves a better fate. Send him away immediately; he is only a fool: but what her mother can mean, Heaven only knows! Good bye," he added, shaking my hand with earnestness; "I do not know when you will see me again; but remember what I tell you of Frederica; you *must* make it your business to see justice done her. She is an amiable girl, and has a very superior mind to what we have given her credit for." He then left me, and ran upstairs. I would not try to stop him, for I know what his feelings must be. The nature of mine, as I listened to him, I need not attempt to describe;

LOVE
AND
FREINDSHIP
AND
OTHER
EARLY
WORKS

for a minute or two I remained in the same spot, overpowered by wonder of a most agreeable sort indeed; yet it required some consideration to be tranquilly happy. In about ten minutes after my return to the parlour Lady Susan entered the room. I concluded, of course, that she and Reginald had been quarrelling; and looked with anxious curiosity for a confirmation of my belief in her face. Mistress of deceit, however, she appeared perfectly unconcerned, and after chatting on indifferent subjects for a short time, said to me, "I find from Wilson that we are going to lose Mr. De Courcy— is it true that he leaves Churchhill this morning?" I replied that it was. "He told us nothing of all this last night," said she, laughing, "or even this morning at breakfast; but perhaps he did not know it himself. Young men are often hasty in their resolutions, and not more sudden in forming than unsteady in keeping them. I should not be surprised if he were to change his mind at last, and not go." She soon afterwards left the room. I trust, however, my dear mother, that we have no reason to fear an alteration of his present plan; things have gone too far. They must have quarrelled, and about Frederica, too. Her calmness astonishes me. What delight will be yours in seeing him again; in seeing him still worthy your esteem, still capable of forming your happiness! When I next write I shall be able to tell you that Sir James is gone, Lady Susan vanquished, and Frederica at peace. We have much to do, but it shall be done. I am all impatience to hear how this astonishing change was effected. I finish as I began, with the warmest congratulations.

Yours ever, etc.,
CATH. VERNON.

•

FROM THE SAME TO THE SAME

Churchhill.

Little did I imagine, my dear Mother, when I sent off my last letter, that the delightful perturbation of spirits I was then in would undergo so speedy, so melancholy a reverse. I never can sufficiently regret that I wrote to you at all. Yet who could have foreseen what has happened? My dear mother, every hope which made me so happy only two hours ago has vanished. The quarrel between Lady Susan and Reginald is made up, and we are all as we were before. One point only is gained. Sir James Martin is dismissed. What are we now to look forward to? I am indeed disappointed; Reginald was all but gone, his horse was ordered and all but brought to the door; who would not have felt safe? For half an hour I was in momentary expectation of his departure. After I had sent off my letter to you, I went to Mr. Vernon, and sat with him in his room talking over the whole matter, and then determined to look for Frederica, whom I had not seen since breakfast. I met her on the stairs, and saw that she was crying. "My dear aunt," said she, "he is going—Mr. De Courcy is going, and it is all my fault. I am afraid you will be very angry with me, but indeed I had no idea it would end so." "My love," I replied, "do not think it necessary to apologize to me on that account. I shall feel myself under an obligation to anyone who is the means of sending my brother home, because," recollecting myself, "I know my father wants very much to see him. But what is it you have done to occasion all this?" She blushed deeply as she answered: "I was so unhappy about Sir James that I could not help—I have done something very wrong, I know; but you have not an idea of the misery I have been in: and mamma had ordered me never to speak to you or my uncle about it, and—" "You therefore spoke to my brother to engage his interference," said I, to save her the explanation. "No, but I wrote to him—I did indeed, I got up this morning before it was light, and was two hours about it; and when my letter was done I thought I never should have courage to give it. After breakfast however, as I was going to my room, I met him in the passage, and then, as I knew that everything must depend on that moment, I forced myself to give it. He was so good as to take it immediately. I dared not look at him, and ran away directly. I was in such a fright I could hardly breathe. My dear aunt, you do not know how miserable I have been." "Frederica" said I, "you ought to have told me all your distresses. You would have found in me a friend always ready to assist you. Do you think that your uncle or I should not have espoused your cause as warmly as my brother?" "Indeed, I did not doubt your kindness," said she, colouring again, "but I thought Mr. De Courcy could do anything with my mother; but I was mistaken: they have had a dreadful quarrel about it, and he is going away.

LOVE
AND
FREINDSHIP
AND
OTHER
EARLY
WORKS

Mamma will never forgive me, and I shall be worse off than ever." "No, you shall not," I replied; "in such a point as this your mother's prohibition ought not to have prevented your speaking to me on the subject. She has no right to make you unhappy, and she shall NOT do it. Your applying, however, to Reginald can be productive only of good to all parties. I believe it is best as it is. Depend upon it that you shall not be made unhappy any longer." At that moment how great was my astonishment at seeing Reginald come out of Lady Susan's dressing-room. My heart misgave me instantly. His confusion at seeing me was very evident. Frederica immediately disappeared. "Are you going?" I said; "you will find Mr. Vernon in his own room." "No, Catherine," he replied, "I am not going. Will you let me speak to you a moment?" We went into my room. "I find," he continued, his confusion increasing as he spoke, "that I have been acting with my usual foolish impetuosity. I have entirely misunderstood Lady Susan, and was on the point of leaving the house under a false impression of her conduct. There has been some very great mistake; we have been all mistaken, I fancy. Frederica does not know her mother. Lady Susan means nothing but her good, but she will not make a friend of her. Lady Susan does not always know, therefore, what will make her daughter happy. Besides, I could have no right to interfere. Miss Vernon was mistaken in applying to me. In short, Catherine, everything has gone wrong, but it is now all happily settled. Lady Susan, I believe, wishes to speak to you about it, if you are at leisure." "Certainly," I replied, deeply sighing at the recital of so lame a story. I made no comments, however, for words would have been vain.

Reginald was glad to get away, and I went to Lady Susan, curious, indeed, to hear her account of it. "Did I not tell you," said she with a smile, "that your brother would not leave us after all?" "You did, indeed," replied I very gravely; "but I flattered myself you would be mistaken." "I should not have hazarded such an opinion," returned she, "if it had not at that moment occurred to me that his resolution of going might be occasioned by a conversation in which we had been this morning engaged, and which had ended very much to his dissatisfaction, from our not rightly understanding each other's meaning. This idea struck me at the moment, and I instantly determined that an accidental dispute, in which I might probably be as much to blame as himself, should not deprive you of your brother. If you remember, I left the room almost immediately. I was resolved to lose no time in clearing up those mistakes as far as I could. The case was this— Frederica had set herself violently against marrying Sir James." "And can your ladyship wonder that she should?" cried I with some warmth; "Frederica has an excellent understanding, and Sir James has none." "I am at least very far from regretting it, my dear sister," said she; "on the contrary, I am grateful for so favourable a sign of my daughter's sense. Sir James is certainly below par (his boyish manners make him appear worse); and had Frederica possessed the penetration and the abilities which I could have wished in my daughter, or had I even known her to possess as much as she does, I should not have been anxious for the match." "It is odd that you should alone be ignorant of your daughter's sense!" "Frederica never does justice to herself; her manners are shy and childish, and besides she is afraid of me. During her poor father's life she was a spoilt child; the severity which it has since been necessary for me to show has alienated her affection; neither has she any of that brilliancy of intellect, that genius or vigour of mind which will force itself forward." "Say rather that she has been unfortunate in her education!" "Heaven knows, my dearest Mrs. Vernon, how fully I am aware of that; but I would wish to forget every circumstance that might throw blame on the memory of one whose name is sacred with me." Here she pretended to cry; I was out of patience with her. "But what," said I, "was your ladyship going to tell me about your disagreement with my brother?" "It originated in an action of my daughter's, which equally marks her want of judgment and the unfortunate dread of me I have been mentioning—she wrote to Mr. De Courcy." "I know she did; you had forbidden her speaking to Mr. Vernon or to me on the cause of her distress; what could she do, therefore, but apply to my brother?" "Good God!" she exclaimed, "what an opinion you must have of me! Can you possibly suppose that I was aware of her unhappiness! that it was my object to make my own child miserable, and that I had forbidden her speaking to you on the subject from a fear of your interrupting the diabolical scheme? Do you think me destitute of every honest, every natural feeling? Am I capable of consigning *her* to everlasting misery whose welfare it is my first earthly duty to promote? The idea is horrible!" "What, then, was your intention when you insisted on her silence?" "Of what use, my

LOVE
AND
FREINDSHIP
AND
OTHER
EARLY
WORKS

dear sister, could be any application to you, however the affair might stand? Why should I subject you to entreaties which I refused to attend to myself? Neither for your sake nor for hers, nor for my own, could such a thing be desirable. When my own resolution was taken I could not wish for the interference, however friendly, of another person. I was mistaken, it is true, but I believed myself right." "But what was this mistake to which your ladyship so often alludes! from whence arose so astonishing a misconception of your daughter's feelings! Did you not know that she disliked Sir James?" "I knew that he was not absolutely the man she would have chosen, but I was persuaded that her objections to him did not arise from any perception of his deficiency. You must not question me, however, my dear sister, too minutely on this point," continued she, taking me affectionately by the hand; "I honestly own that there is something to conceal. Frederica makes me very unhappy! Her applying to Mr. De Courcy hurt me particularly." "What is it you mean to infer," said I, "by this appearance of mystery? If you think your daughter at all attached to Reginald, her objecting to Sir James could not less deserve to be attended to than if the cause of her objecting had been a consciousness of his folly; and why should your ladyship, at any rate, quarrel with my brother for an interference which, you must know, it is not in his nature to refuse when urged in such a manner?"

"His disposition, you know, is warm, and he came to expostulate with me; his compassion all alive for this ill-used girl, this heroine in distress! We misunderstood each other: he believed me more to blame than I really was; I considered his interference less excusable than I now find it. I have a real regard for him, and was beyond expression mortified to find it, as I thought, so ill bestowed. We were both warm, and of course both to blame. His resolution of leaving Churchhill is consistent with his general eagerness. When I understood his intention, however, and at the same time began to think that we had been perhaps equally mistaken in each other's meaning, I resolved to have an explanation before it was too late. For any member of your family I must always feel a degree of affection, and I own it would have sensibly hurt me if my acquaintance with Mr. De Courcy had ended so gloomily. I have now only to say further, that as I am convinced of Frederica's having a reasonable dislike to Sir James, I shall instantly inform him that he must give up all hope of her.

I reproach myself for having, even though innocently, made her unhappy on that score. She shall have all the retribution in my power to make; if she value her own happiness as much as I do, if she judge wisely, and command herself as she ought, she may now be easy. Excuse me, my dearest sister, for thus trespassing on your time, but I owe it to my own character; and after this explanation I trust I am in no danger of sinking in your opinion." I could have said, "Not much, indeed!" but I left her almost in silence. It was the greatest stretch of forbearance I could practise. I could not have stopped myself had I begun. Her assurance! her deceit! but I will not allow myself to dwell on them; they will strike you sufficiently. My heart sickens within me. As soon as I was tolerably composed I returned to the parlour. Sir James's carriage was at the door, and he, merry as usual, soon afterwards took his leave. How easily does her ladyship encourage or dismiss a lover! In spite of this release, Frederica still looks unhappy: still fearful, perhaps, of her mother's anger; and though dreading my brother's departure, jealous, it may be, of his staying. I see how closely she observes him and Lady Susan, poor girl! I have now no hope for her. There is not a chance of her affection being returned. He thinks very differently of her from what he used to do; he does her some justice, but his reconciliation with her mother precludes every dearer hope. Prepare, my dear mother, for the worst! The probability of their marrying is surely heightened! He is more securely hers than ever. When that wretched event takes place, Frederica must belong wholly to us. I am thankful that my last letter will precede this by so little, as every moment that you can be saved from feeling a joy which leads only to disappointment is of consequence.

Yours ever, etc.,
CATHERINE VERNON.

•

LADY SUSAN TO MRS. JOHNSON

Churchhill.

I call on you, dear Alicia, for congratulations: I am my own self, gay and triumphant! When I wrote to you the other day I was, in truth, in high irritation, and with ample cause. Nay, I know not whether I ought to be quite tranquil now, for I have had more trouble in restoring peace than I ever intended to submit to—a spirit, too, resulting from a fancied sense of superior integrity, which is peculiarly insolent! I shall not easily forgive him, I assure you. He was actually on the point of leaving Churchhill! I had scarcely concluded my last, when Wilson brought me word of it. I found, therefore, that something must be done; for I did not choose to leave my character at the mercy of a man whose passions are so violent and so revengeful. It would have been trifling with my reputation to allow of his departing with such an impression in my disfavour; in this light, condescension was necessary. I sent Wilson to say that I desired to speak with him before he went; he came immediately. The angry emotions which had marked every feature when we last parted were partially subdued. He seemed astonished at the summons, and looked as if half wishing and half fearing to be softened by what I might say. If my countenance expressed what I aimed at, it was composed and dignified; and yet, with a degree of pensiveness which might convince him that I was not quite happy. "I beg your pardon, sir, for the liberty I have taken in sending for you," said I; "but as I have just learnt your intention of leaving this place to-day, I feel it my duty to entreat that you will not on my account shorten your visit here even an hour. I am perfectly aware that after what has passed between us it would ill suit the feelings of either to remain longer in the same house: so very great, so total a change from the intimacy of friendship must render any future intercourse the severest punishment; and your resolution of quitting Churchhill is undoubtedly in unison with our situation, and with those lively feelings which I know you to possess. But, at the same time, it is not for me to suffer such a sacrifice as it must be to leave relations to whom you are so much attached, and are so dear. My remaining here cannot give that pleasure to Mr. and Mrs. Vernon which your society must; and my visit has already perhaps been too long. My removal, therefore, which must, at any rate, take place soon, may, with perfect convenience, be hastened; and I make it my particular request that I may not in any way be instrumental in separating a family so affectionately attached to each other. Where I go is of no consequence to anyone; of very little to myself; but you are of importance to all your connections." Here I concluded, and I hope you will be satisfied with my speech. Its effect on Reginald justifies some portion of vanity, for it was no less favourable than instantaneous. Oh, how delightful it was to watch the variations of his countenance while I spoke! to see the struggle between returning tenderness and the remains of displeasure. There is something agreeable in feelings so easily worked on; not that I envy him their possession, nor would, for the world, have such myself; but they are very convenient when one wishes to influence the passions of another. And yet this Reginald, whom a very few words from me softened at once into the utmost submission, and rendered more tractable, more attached, more devoted than ever, would have left me in the first angry swelling of his proud heart without deigning to seek an explanation. Humbled as he now is, I cannot forgive him such an instance of pride, and am doubtful whether I ought not to punish him by dismissing him at once after this reconciliation, or by marrying and teazing him for ever. But these measures are each too violent to be adopted without some deliberation; at present my thoughts are fluctuating between various schemes. I have many things to compass: I must punish Frederica, and pretty severely too, for her application to Reginald; I must punish him for receiving it so favourably, and for the rest of his conduct. I must torment my sister-in-law for the insolent triumph of her look and manner since Sir James has been dismissed; for, in reconciling Reginald to me, I was not able to save that ill-fated young man; and I must make myself amends for the humiliation to which I have stooped within these few days. To effect all this I have various plans. I have also an idea of being soon in town; and whatever may be my determination as to the rest, I shall probably put *that* project in execution; for London will be always the fairest field of action, however my views may be directed; and at any rate I shall there be rewarded by your society, and a little dissipation, for a ten weeks' penance at Churchhill. I believe I owe it to my character to complete the match between my daughter and Sir James after having so long intended it. Let me know your opinion on this point. Flexibility of mind, a disposition easily biassed by others, is an attribute which you know I am not very desirous of obtaining; nor has Frederica any claim to the indulgence of her notions at the expense of her mother's inclinations. Her idle love for Reginald, too! It is surely my duty to discourage such romantic nonsense. All things considered,

LOVE
AND
FREINDSHIP
AND
OTHER
EARLY
WORKS

therefore, it seems incumbent on me to take her to town and marry her immediately to Sir James. When my own will is effected contrary to his, I shall have some credit in being on good terms with Reginald, which at present, in fact, I have not; for though he is still in my power, I have given up the very article by which our quarrel was produced, and at best the honour of victory is doubtful. Send me your opinion on all these matters, my dear Alicia, and let me know whether you can get lodgings to suit me within a short distance of you.

Your most attached
S. VERNON.

•

MRS. JOHNSON TO LADY SUSAN

Edward Street.

I am gratified by your reference, and this is my advice: that you come to town yourself, without loss of time, but that you leave Frederica behind. It would surely be much more to the purpose to get yourself well established by marrying Mr. De Courcy, than to irritate him and the rest of his family by making her marry Sir James. You should think more of yourself and less of your daughter. She is not of a disposition to do you credit in the world, and seems precisely in her proper place at Churchhill, with the Vernons. But you are fitted for society, and it is shameful to have you exiled from it. Leave Frederica, therefore, to punish herself for the plague she has given you, by indulging that romantic tender-heartedness which will always ensure her misery enough, and come to London as soon as you can. I have another reason for urging this: Mainwaring came to town last week, and has contrived, in spite of Mr. Johnson, to make opportunities of seeing me. He is absolutely miserable about you, and jealous to such a degree of De Courcy that it would be highly unadvisable for them to meet at present. And yet, if you do not allow him to see you here, I cannot answer for his not committing some great imprudence—such as going to Churchhill, for instance, which would be dreadful! Besides, if you take my advice, and resolve to marry De Courcy, it will be indispensably necessary to you to get Mainwaring out of the way; and you only can have influence enough to send him back to his wife. I have still another motive for your coming: Mr. Johnson leaves London next Tuesday; he is going for his health to Bath, where, if the waters are favourable to his constitution and my wishes, he will be laid up with the gout many weeks. During his absence we shall be able to chuse our own society, and to have true enjoyment. I would ask you to Edward Street, but that once he forced from me a kind of promise never to invite you to my house; nothing but my being in the utmost distress for money should have extorted it from me. I can get you, however, a nice drawing-room apartment in Upper Seymour Street, and we may be always together there or here; for I consider my promise to Mr. Johnson as comprehending only (at least in his absence) your not sleeping in the house. Poor Mainwaring gives me such histories of his wife's jealousy. Silly woman to expect constancy from so charming a man! but she always was silly—intolerably so in marrying him at all, she the heiress of a large fortune and he without a shilling: one title, I know, she might have had, besides baronets. Her folly in forming the connection was so great that, though Mr. Johnson was her guardian, and I do not in general share HIS feelings, I never can forgive her.

Adieu. Yours ever,
ALICIA.

●

MRS. VERNON TO LADY DE COURCY

Churchhill.

This letter, my dear Mother, will be brought you by Reginald. His long visit is about to be concluded at last, but I fear the separation takes place too late to do us any good. She is going to London to see her particular friend, Mrs. Johnson. It was at first her intention that Frederica should accompany her, for the benefit of masters, but we overruled her there. Frederica was wretched in the idea of going, and I could not bear to have her at the mercy of her mother; not all the masters in London could compensate for the ruin of her comfort. I should have feared, too, for her health, and for everything but her principles—there I believe she is not to be injured by

LOVE
AND
FREINDSHIP
AND
OTHER
EARLY
WORKS

her mother, or her mother's friends; but with those friends she must have mixed (a very bad set, I doubt not), or have been left in total solitude, and I can hardly tell which would have been worse for her. If she is with her mother, moreover, she must, alas! in all probability be with Reginald, and that would be the greatest evil of all. Here we shall in time be in peace, and our regular employments, our books and conversations, with exercise, the children, and every domestic pleasure in my power to procure her, will, I trust, gradually overcome this youthful attachment. I should not have a doubt of it were she slighted for any other woman in the world than her own mother. How long Lady Susan will be in town, or whether she returns here again, I know not. I could not be cordial in my invitation, but if she chuses to come no want of cordiality on my part will keep her away. I could not help asking Reginald if he intended being in London this winter, as soon as I found her ladyship's steps would be bent thither; and though he professed himself quite undetermined, there was something in his look and voice as he spoke which contradicted his words. I have done with lamentation; I look upon the event as so far decided that I resign myself to it in despair. If he leaves you soon for London everything will be concluded.

Your affectionate, etc.,
C. VERNON.

●

MRS. JOHNSON TO LADY SUSAN

Edward Street.

My dearest Friend,—I write in the greatest distress; the most unfortunate event has just taken place. Mr. Johnson has hit on the most effectual manner of plaguing us all. He had heard, I imagine, by some means or other, that you were soon to be in London, and immediately contrived to have such an attack of the gout as must at least delay his journey to Bath, if not wholly prevent it. I am persuaded the gout is brought on or kept off at pleasure; it was the same when I wanted to join the Hamiltons to the Lakes; and three years ago, when I had a fancy for Bath, nothing could induce him to have a gouty symptom.

I am pleased to find that my letter had so much effect on you, and that De Courcy is certainly your own. Let me hear from you as soon as you arrive, and in particular tell me what you mean to do with Mainwaring. It is impossible to say when I shall be able to come to you; my confinement must be great. It is such an abominable trick to be ill here instead of at Bath that I can scarcely command myself at all. At Bath his old aunts would have nursed him, but here it all falls upon me; and he bears pain with such patience that I have not the common excuse for losing my temper.

Yours ever,
ALICIA.

•

LADY SUSAN VERNON TO MRS. JOHNSON

Upper Seymour Street.

My dear Alicia,—There needed not this last fit of the gout to make me detest Mr. Johnson, but now the extent of my aversion is not to be estimated. To have you confined as nurse in his apartment! My dear Alicia, of what a mistake were you guilty in marrying a man of his age! just old enough to be formal, ungovernable, and to have the gout; too old to be agreeable, too young to die. I arrived last night about five, had scarcely swallowed my dinner when Mainwaring made his appearance. I will not dissemble what real pleasure his sight afforded me, nor how strongly I felt the contrast between his person and manners and those of Reginald, to the infinite disadvantage of the latter. For an hour or two I was even staggered in my resolution of marrying him, and though this was too idle and nonsensical an idea to remain long on my mind, I do not feel very eager for the conclusion of my marriage, nor look forward with much impatience to the time when Reginald, according to our agreement, is to be in town. I shall probably put off his arrival under some pretence or other. He must not come till Mainwaring is gone. I am still doubtful at times as to marrying; if the old man would die I might not hesitate, but a state of dependance on the caprice of Sir Reginald will not suit the freedom of my spirit; and if I resolve to wait for that event, I shall have excuse enough at

LOVE
AND
FREINDSHIP
AND
OTHER
EARLY
WORKS

present in having been scarcely ten months a widow. I have not given Mainwaring any hint of my intention, or allowed him to consider my acquaintance with Reginald as more than the commonest flirtation, and he is tolerably appeased. Adieu, till we meet; I am enchanted with my lodgings.

Yours ever,
S. VERNON.

●

LADY SUSAN VERNON TO MR. DE COURCY

Upper Seymour Street.

I have received your letter, and though I do not attempt to conceal that I am gratified by your impatience for the hour of meeting, I yet feel myself under the necessity of delaying that hour beyond the time originally fixed. Do not think me unkind for such an exercise of my power, nor accuse me of instability without first hearing my reasons. In the course of my journey from Churchhill I had ample leisure for reflection on the present state of our affairs, and every review has served to convince me that they require a delicacy and cautiousness of conduct to which we have hitherto been too little attentive. We have been hurried on by our feelings to a degree of precipitation which ill accords with the claims of our friends or the opinion of the world. We have been unguarded in forming this hasty engagement, but we must not complete the imprudence by ratifying it while there is so much reason to fear the connection would be opposed by those friends on whom you depend. It is not for us to blame any expectations on your father's side of your marrying to advantage; where possessions are so extensive as those of your family, the wish of increasing them, if not strictly reasonable, is too common to excite surprize or resentment. He has a right to require; a woman of fortune in his daughter-in-law, and I am sometimes quarrelling with myself for suffering you to form a connection so imprudent; but the influence of reason is often acknowledged too late by those who feel like me. I have now been but a few months a widow, and, however little indebted to my husband's memory for any happiness derived from him during a union of some years, I cannot forget that the indelicacy of so early a second marriage must subject me to the censure of the world, and incur, what would be still more insupportable, the displeasure of Mr. Vernon. I might perhaps harden myself in time against the injustice of general reproach, but the loss of HIS valued esteem I am, as you well know, ill-fitted to endure; and when to this may be added the consciousness of having injured you with your family, how am I to support myself? With feelings so poignant as mine, the conviction of having divided the son from his parents would make me, even with you, the most miserable of beings. It will surely, therefore, be advisable to delay our union—to delay it till appearances are more promising—till affairs have taken a more favourable turn. To assist us in such a resolution I feel that absence will be necessary. We must not meet. Cruel as this sentence may appear, the necessity of pronouncing it, which can alone reconcile it to myself, will be evident to you when you have considered our situation in the light in which I have found myself imperiously obliged to place it. You may be—you must be—well assured that nothing but the strongest conviction of duty could induce me to wound my own feelings by urging a lengthened separation, and of insensibility to yours you will hardly suspect me. Again, therefore, I say that we ought not, we must not, yet meet. By a removal for some months from each other we shall tranquillise the sisterly fears of Mrs. Vernon, who, accustomed herself to the enjoyment of riches, considers fortune as necessary everywhere, and whose sensibilities are not of a nature to comprehend ours. Let me hear from you soon—very soon. Tell me that you submit to my arguments, and do not reproach me for using such. I cannot bear reproaches: my spirits are not so high as to need being repressed. I must endeavour to seek amusement, and fortunately many of my friends are in town; amongst them the Mainwarings; you know how sincerely I regard both husband and wife.

I am, very faithfully yours,
S. VERNON

●

LOVE
AND
FREINDSHIP
AND
OTHER
EARLY
WORKS

LADY SUSAN TO MRS. JOHNSON

Upper Seymour Street.

My dear Friend,—

That tormenting creature, Reginald, is here. My letter, which was intended to keep him longer in the country, has hastened him to town. Much as I wish him away, however, I cannot help being pleased with such a proof of attachment. He is devoted to me, heart and soul. He will carry this note himself, which is to serve as an introduction to you, with whom he longs to be acquainted. Allow him to spend the evening with you, that I may be in no danger of his returning here. I have told him that I am not quite well, and must be alone; and should he call again there might be confusion, for it is impossible to be sure of servants. Keep him, therefore, I entreat you, in Edward Street. You will not find him a heavy companion, and I allow you to flirt with him as much as you like. At the same time, do not forget my real interest; say all that you can to convince him that I shall be quite wretched if he remains here; you know my reasons—propriety, and so forth. I would urge them more myself, but that I am impatient to be rid of him, as Mainwaring comes within half an hour.

Adieu!
S. VERNON

●

MRS. JOHNSON TO LADY SUSAN

Edward Street.

My dear Creature,—

I am in agonies, and know not what to do. Mr. De Courcy arrived just when he should not. Mrs. Mainwaring had that instant entered the house, and forced herself into her guardian's presence, though I did not know a syllable of it till afterwards, for I was out when both she and Reginald came, or I should have sent him away at all events; but she was shut up with Mr. Johnson, while he waited in the drawing-room for me. She arrived yesterday in pursuit of her husband, but perhaps you know this already from himself. She came to this house to entreat my husband's interference, and before I could be aware of it, everything that you could wish to be concealed was known to him, and unluckily she had wormed out of Mainwaring's servant that he had visited you every day since your being in town, and had just watched him to your door herself! What could I do! Facts are such horrid things! All is by this time known to De Courcy, who is now alone with Mr. Johnson. Do not accuse me; indeed, it was impossible to prevent it. Mr. Johnson has for some time suspected De Courcy of intending to marry you, and would speak with him alone as soon as he knew him to be in the house. That detestable Mrs. Mainwaring, who, for your comfort, has fretted herself thinner and uglier than ever, is still here, and they have been all closeted together. What can be done? At any rate, I hope he will plague his wife more than ever.

With anxious wishes,
Yours faithfully,
ALICIA.

●

LADY SUSAN TO MRS. JOHNSON

Upper Seymour Street.

This eclaircissement is rather provoking. How unlucky that you should have been from home! I thought myself sure of you at seven! I am undismayed however. Do not torment yourself with fears on my account; depend on it, I can make my story good with Reginald. Mainwaring is just gone; he brought me the news of his wife's arrival. Silly woman, what does she expect by such manoeuvres? Yet I wish she had stayed quietly at Langford. Reginald will be a little enraged at first, but by to-morrow's dinner, everything will be well again.

Adieu!
S. V.

●

MR. DE COURCY TO LADY SUSAN

LOVE
AND
FREINDSHIP
AND
OTHER
EARLY
WORKS

—Hotel

I write only to bid you farewell, the spell is removed; I see you as you are. Since we parted yesterday, I have received from indisputable authority such a history of you as must bring the most mortifying conviction of the imposition I have been under, and the absolute necessity of an immediate and eternal separation from you. You cannot doubt to what I allude. Langford! Langford! that word will be sufficient. I received my information in Mr. Johnson's house, from Mrs. Mainwaring herself. You know how I have loved you; you can intimately judge of my present feelings, but I am not so weak as to find indulgence in describing them to a woman who will glory in having excited their anguish, but whose affection they have never been able to gain.

R. DE COURCY.

●

LADY SUSAN TO MR. DE COURCY

Upper Seymour Street.

I will not attempt to describe my astonishment in reading the note this moment received from you. I am bewildered in my endeavours to form some rational conjecture of what Mrs. Mainwaring can have told you to occasion so extraordinary a change in your sentiments. Have I not explained everything to you with respect to myself which could bear a doubtful meaning, and which the ill-nature of the world had interpreted to my discredit? What can you now have heard to stagger your esteem for me? Have I ever had a concealment from you? Reginald, you agitate me beyond expression, I cannot suppose that the old story of Mrs. Mainwaring's jealousy can be revived again, or at least be LISTENED to again. Come to me immediately, and explain what is at present absolutely incomprehensible. Believe me the single word of Langford is not of such potent intelligence as to supersede the necessity of more. If we ARE to part, it will at least be handsome to take your personal leave—but I have little heart to jest; in truth, I am serious enough; for to be sunk, though but for an hour, in your esteem is a humiliation to which I know not how to submit. I shall count every minute till your arrival.

S. V.

●

—Hotel.

Why would you write to me? Why do you require particulars? But, since it must be so, I am obliged to declare that all the accounts of your misconduct during the life, and since the death of Mr. Vernon, which had reached me, in common with the world in general, and gained my entire belief before I saw you, but which you, by the exertion of your perverted abilities, had made me resolved to disallow, have been unanswerably proved to me; nay more, I am assured that a connection, of which I had never before entertained a thought, has for some time existed, and still continues to exist, between you and the man whose family you robbed of its peace in return for the hospitality with which you were received into it; that you have corresponded with him ever since your leaving Langford; not with his wife, but with him, and that he now visits you every day. Can you, dare you deny it? and all this at the time when I was an encouraged, an accepted lover! From what have I not escaped! I have only to be grateful. Far from me be all complaint, every sigh of regret. My own folly had endangered me, my preservation I owe to the kindness, the integrity of another; but the unfortunate Mrs. Mainwaring, whose agonies while she related the past seemed to threaten her reason, how is SHE to be consoled! After such a discovery as this, you will scarcely affect further wonder at my meaning in bidding you adieu. My understanding is at length restored, and teaches no less to abhor the artifices which had subdued me than to despise myself for the weakness on which their strength was founded.

R. DE COURCY.

•

LADY SUSAN TO MR. DE COURCY

Upper Seymour Street.

LOVE
AND
FREINDSHIP
AND
OTHER
EARLY
WORKS

I am satisfied, and will trouble you no more when these few lines are dismissed. The engagement which you were eager to form a fortnight ago is no longer compatible with your views, and I rejoice to find that the prudent advice of your parents has not been given in vain. Your restoration to peace will, I doubt not, speedily follow this act of filial obedience, and I flatter myself with the hope of surviving my share in this disappointment.

S. V.

●

MRS. JOHNSON TO LADY SUSAN VERNON

Edward Street

I am grieved, though I cannot be astonished at your rupture with Mr. De Courcy; he has just informed Mr. Johnson of it by letter. He leaves London, he says, to-day. Be assured that I partake in all your feelings, and do not be angry if I say that our intercourse, even by letter, must soon be given up. It makes me miserable; but Mr. Johnson vows that if I persist in the connection, he will settle in the country for the rest of his life, and you know it is impossible to submit to such an extremity while any other alternative remains. You have heard of course that the Mainwarings are to part, and I am afraid Mrs. M. will come home to us again; but she is still so fond of her husband, and frets so much about him, that perhaps she may not live long. Miss Mainwaring is just come to town to be with her aunt, and they say that she declares she will have Sir James Martin before she leaves London again. If I were you, I would certainly get him myself. I had almost forgot to give you my opinion of Mr. De Courcy; I am really delighted with him; he is full as handsome, I think, as Mainwaring, and with such an open, good-humoured countenance, that one cannot help loving him at first sight. Mr. Johnson and he are the greatest friends in the world. Adieu, my dearest Susan, I wish matters did not go so perversely. That unlucky visit to Langford! but I dare say you did all for the best, and there is no defying destiny.

Your sincerely attached
ALICIA.

●

LADY SUSAN TO MRS. JOHNSON

Upper Seymour Street.

My dear Alicia,—

I yield to the necessity which parts us. Under circumstances you could not act otherwise. Our friendship cannot be impaired by it, and in happier times, when your situation is as independent as mine, it will unite us again in the same intimacy as ever. For this I shall impatiently wait, and meanwhile can safely assure you that I never was more at ease, or better satisfied with myself and everything about me than at the present hour. Your husband I abhor, Reginald I despise, and I am secure of never seeing either again. Have I not reason to rejoice? Mainwaring is more devoted to me than ever; and were we at liberty, I doubt if I could resist even matrimony offered by HIM. This event, if his wife live with you, it may be in your power to hasten. The violence of her feelings, which must wear her out, may be easily kept in irritation. I rely on your friendship for this. I am now satisfied that I never could have brought myself to marry Reginald, and am equally determined that Frederica never shall. To-morrow, I shall fetch her from Churchhill, and let Maria Mainwaring tremble for the consequence. Frederica shall be Sir James's wife before she quits my house, and she may whimper, and the Vernons may storm, I regard them not. I am tired of submitting my will to the caprices of others; of resigning my own judgment in deference to those to whom I owe no duty, and for whom I feel no respect. I have given up too much, have been too easily worked on, but Frederica shall now feel the difference.

Adieu, dearest of friends; may the next gouty attack be more favourable! and may you always regard me as unalterably yours,

S. VERNON

●

LADY DE COURCY TO MRS. VERNON

LOVE
AND
FREINDSHIP
AND
OTHER
EARLY
WORKS

My dear Catherine,—

I have charming news for you, and if I had not sent off my letter this morning you might have been spared the vexation of know-ing of Reginald's being gone to London, for he is returned. Reginald is returned, not to ask our consent to his marrying Lady Susan, but to tell us they are parted for ever. He has been only an hour in the house, and I have not been able to learn particulars, for he is so very low that I have not the heart to ask questions, but I hope we shall soon know all. This is the most joyful hour he has ever given us since the day of his birth. Nothing is wanting but to have you here, and it is our particular wish and entreaty that you would come to us as soon as you can. You have owed us a visit many long weeks; I hope nothing will make it inconvenient to Mr. Vernon; and pray bring all my grand-children; and your dear niece is included, of course; I long to see her. It has been a sad, heavy winter hitherto, without Reginald, and seeing nobody from Churchhill. I never found the season so dreary before; but this happy meeting will make us young again. Frederica runs much in my thoughts, and when Reginald has recovered his usual good spirits (as I trust he soon will) we will try to rob him of his heart once more, and I am full of hopes of seeing their hands joined at no great distance.

Your affectionate mother,
C. DE COURCY

●

MRS. VERNON TO LADY DE COURCY

Churchhill.

My dear Mother,—
Your letter has surprized me beyond measure! Can it be true that they are really separated—and for ever? I should be overjoyed if I dared depend on it, but after all that I have seen how can one be secure. And Reginald really with you! My surprize is the greater because on Wednesday, the very day of his coming to Parklands, we had a most unexpected and unwelcome visit from Lady Susan, looking all cheerfulness and good-humour, and seeming more as if she were to marry him when she got to London than as if parted from him for ever. She stayed nearly two hours, was as affectionate and agreeable as ever, and not a syllable, not a hint was dropped, of any disagreement or coolness between them. I asked her

whether she had seen my brother since his arrival in town; not, as you may suppose, with any doubt of the fact, but merely to see how she looked. She immediately answered, without any embarrassment, that he had been kind enough to call on her on Monday; but she believed he had already returned home, which I was very far from crediting. Your kind invitation is accepted by us with pleasure, and on Thursday next we and our little ones will be with you. Pray heaven, Reginald may not be in town again by that time! I wish we could bring dear Frederica too, but I am sorry to say that her mother's errand hither was to fetch her away; and, miserable as it made the poor girl, it was impossible to detain her. I was thoroughly unwilling to let her go, and so was her uncle; and all that could be urged we did urge; but Lady Susan declared that as she was now about to fix herself in London for several months, she could not be easy if her daughter were not with her for masters, etc. Her manner, to be sure, was very kind and proper, and Mr. Vernon believes that Frederica will now be treated with affection. I wish I could think so too. The poor girl's heart was almost broke at taking leave of us. I charged her to write to me very often, and to remember that if she were in any distress we should be always her friends. I took care to see her alone, that I might say all this, and I hope made her a little more comfortable; but I shall not be easy till I can go to town and judge of her situation myself. I wish there were a better prospect than now appears of the match which the conclusion of your letter declares your expectations of. At present, it is not very likely,

Yours ever, etc.,
C. VERNON

●

LOVE
AND
FREINDSHIP
AND
OTHER
EARLY
WORKS

This correspondence, by a meeting between some of the parties, and a separation between the others, could not, to the great detriment of the Post Office revenue, be continued any longer. Very little assistance to the State could be derived from the epistolary intercourse of Mrs. Vernon and her niece; for the former soon perceived, by the style of Frederica's letters, that they were written under her mother's inspection! and therefore, deferring all particular enquiry till she could make it personally in London, ceased writing minutely or often. Having learnt enough, in the meanwhile, from her open-hearted brother, of what had passed between him and Lady Susan to sink the latter lower than ever in her opinion, she was proportionably more anxious to get Frederica removed from such a mother, and placed under her own care; and, though with little hope of success, was resolved to leave nothing unattempted that might offer a chance of obtaining her sister-in-law's consent to it. Her anxiety on the subject made her press for an early visit to London; and Mr. Vernon, who, as it must already have appeared, lived only to do whatever he was desired, soon found some accommodating business to call him thither. With a heart full of the matter, Mrs. Vernon waited on Lady Susan shortly after her arrival in town, and was met with such an easy and cheerful affection, as made her almost turn from her with horror. No remembrance of Reginald, no consciousness of guilt, gave one look of embarrassment; she was in excellent spirits, and seemed eager to show at once by ever possible attention to her brother and sister her sense of their kindness, and her pleasure in their society. Frederica was no more altered than Lady Susan; the same restrained manners, the same timid look in the presence of her mother as heretofore, assured her aunt of her situation being uncomfortable, and confirmed her in the plan of altering it. No unkindness, however, on the part of Lady Susan appeared. Persecution on the subject of Sir James was entirely at an end; his name merely mentioned to say that he was not in London; and indeed, in all her conversation, she was solicitous only for the welfare and improvement of her daughter, acknowledging, in terms of grateful delight, that Frederica was now growing every day more and more what a parent could desire. Mrs. Vernon, surprized and incredulous, knew not what to suspect, and, without any change in her own views, only feared greater difficulty in accomplishing them. The first hope of anything better was derived from Lady Susan's asking her whether she thought Frederica looked quite as well as she had done at Churchhill, as she must confess herself to have sometimes an anxious doubt of London's perfectly agreeing with her. Mrs. Vernon, encouraging the doubt, directly proposed her niece's returning with them into the country. Lady Susan was unable to express her sense of such kindness, yet knew not, from a variety of reasons, how to part with her daughter; and as, though her own plans were not yet wholly fixed, she trusted it would ere long be in her power to take Frederica into the country herself, concluded by declining entirely to profit by such unexampled attention. Mrs. Vernon persevered, however, in the offer of it, and though Lady Susan continued to resist, her resistance in the course of a few days seemed somewhat less formidable. The lucky alarm of an influenza decided what might not have been decided quite so soon. Lady Susan's maternal fears were then too much awakened for her to think of anything but Frederica's removal from the risk of infection; above all disorders in the world she most dreaded the influenza for her daughter's constitution!

Frederica returned to Churchhill with her uncle and aunt; and three weeks afterwards, Lady Susan announced her being married to Sir James Martin. Mrs. Vernon was then convinced of what she had only suspected before, that she might have spared herself all the trouble of urging a removal which Lady Susan had doubtless resolved on from the first. Frederica's visit was nominally for six weeks, but her mother, though inviting her to return in one or two affectionate letters, was very ready to oblige the whole party by consenting to a prolongation of her stay, and in the course of two months ceased to write of her absence, and in the course of two or more to write to her at all. Frederica was therefore fixed in the family of her uncle and aunt till such time as Reginald De Courcy could be talked, flattered, and finessed into an affection for her which, allowing leisure for the conquest of his attachment to her mother, for his abjuring all future attachments, and detesting the sex, might be reasonably looked for in the course of a twelvemonth. Three months might have done it in general, but Reginald's feelings were no less lasting than lively. Whether Lady Susan was or was not happy in her second choice, I do not see how it can ever be ascertained; for who would take her assurance of it on either side of the question? The world must judge from probabilities; she had nothing against her but her husband, and her conscience. Sir James may seem to have drawn a harder lot than mere folly merited; I leave him, therefore, to all the pity that anybody can give him. For myself, I confess that I can pity only Miss Mainwaring; who, coming to town, and putting herself to an expense in clothes which impoverished her for two years, on purpose to secure him, was defrauded of her due by a woman ten years older than herself.

PART

IV

THE HISTORY OF ENGLAND: FROM THE REIGN OF HENRY THE 4TH TO THE DEATH OF CHARLES THE 1ST

BY A PARTIAL, PREJUDICED, AND IGNORANT HISTORIAN.

N.B. There will be very few Dates in this History.

HENRY the 4th

Henry the 4th ascended the throne of England much to his own satisfaction in the year 1399, after having prevailed on his cousin and predecessor Richard the 2nd, to resign it to him, and to retire for the rest of his life to Pomfret Castle, where he happened to be murdered. It is to be supposed that Henry was married, since he had certainly four sons, but it is not in my power to inform the Reader who was his wife. Be this as it may, he did not live for ever, but falling ill, his son the Prince of Wales came and took away the crown; whereupon the King made a long speech, for which I must refer the Reader to Shakespear's Plays, and the Prince made a still longer. Things being thus settled between them the King died, and was succeeded by his son Henry who had previously beat Sir William Gascoigne.

HENRY the 5th

This Prince after he succeeded to the throne grew quite reformed and amiable, forsaking all his dissipated companions, and never thrashing Sir William again. During his reign, Lord Cobham was burnt alive, but I forget what for. His Majesty then turned his thoughts to France, where he went and fought the famous Battle of Agincourt. He afterwards married the King's daughter Catherine, a very agreable woman by Shakespear's account. In spite of all this however he died, and was succeeded by his son Henry.

HENRY the 6th

I cannot say much for this Monarch's sense. Nor would I if I could, for he was a Lancastrian. I suppose you know all about the Wars between him and the Duke of York who was of the right side; if you do not, you had better read some other History, for I shall not be very diffuse in this, meaning by it only to vent my spleen *against*, and shew my Hatred *to* all those people whose parties or principles do not suit with mine, and not to give information. This King married Margaret of Anjou, a Woman whose distresses and misfortunes were so great as almost to make me who hate her, pity her. It was in this reign that Joan of Arc lived and made such a *row* among the English. They should not have burnt her—but they did. There were several Battles between the Yorkists and Lancastrians, in which the former (as they ought) usually conquered. At length they were entirely overcome; The King was murdered—The Queen was sent home—and Edward the 4th ascended the Throne.

EDWARD the 4th

This Monarch was famous only for his Beauty and his Courage, of which the Picture we have here given of him, and his undaunted Behaviour in marrying one Woman while he was engaged to another, are sufficient proofs. His Wife was Elizabeth Woodville, a Widow who, poor Woman! was afterwards confined in a Convent by that Monster of Iniquity and Avarice Henry the 7th. One of Edward's Mistresses was Jane Shore, who has had a play written about her, but it is a tragedy and therefore not worth reading. Having performed all these noble actions, his Majesty died, and was succeeded by his son.

EDWARD the 5th

This unfortunate Prince lived so little a while that nobody had him to draw his picture. He was murdered by his Uncle's Contrivance, whose name was Richard the 3rd.

RICHARD the 3rd

LOVE
AND
FREINDSHIP
AND
OTHER
EARLY
WORKS

The Character of this Prince has been in general very severely treated by Historians, but as he was a YORK, I am rather inclined to suppose him a very respectable Man. It has indeed been confidently asserted that he killed his two Nephews and his Wife, but it has also been declared that he did not kill his two Nephews, which I am inclined to beleive true; and if this is the case, it may also be affirmed that he did not kill his Wife, for if Perkin Warbeck was really the Duke of York, why might not Lambert Simnel be the Widow of Richard. Whether innocent or guilty, he did not reign long in peace, for Henry Tudor E. of Richmond as great a villain as ever lived, made a great fuss about getting the Crown and having killed the King at the battle of Bosworth, he succeeded to it.

HENRY the 7th

This Monarch soon after his accession married the Princess Elizabeth of York, by which alliance he plainly proved that he thought his own right inferior to hers, tho' he pretended to the contrary. By this Marriage he had two sons and two daughters, the elder of which Daughters was married to the King of Scotland and had the happiness of being grandmother to one of the first Characters in the World. But of HER, I shall have occasion to speak more at large in future. The youngest, Mary, married first the King of France and secondly the D. of Suffolk, by whom she had one daughter, afterwards the Mother of Lady Jane Grey, who tho' inferior to her lovely Cousin the Queen of Scots, was yet an amiable young woman and famous for reading Greek while other people were hunting. It was in the reign of Henry the 7th that Perkin Warbeck and Lambert Simnel before mentioned made their appearance, the former of whom was set in the stocks, took shelter in Beaulieu Abbey, and was beheaded with the Earl of Warwick, and the latter was taken into the Kings kitchen. His Majesty died and was succeeded by his son Henry whose only merit was his not being quite so bad as his daughter Elizabeth.

HENRY the 8th

It would be an affront to my Readers were I to suppose that they were not as well acquainted with the particulars of this King's reign as I am myself. It will therefore be saving *them* the task of reading again what they have read before, and *myself* the trouble of writing what I do not perfectly recollect, by giving only a slight sketch of the principal Events which marked his reign. Among these may be ranked Cardinal Wolsey's telling the father Abbott of Leicester Abbey that "he was come to lay his bones among them," the reformation in Religion and the King's riding through the streets of London with Anna Bullen. It is however but

Justice, and my Duty to declare that this amiable Woman was entirely innocent of the Crimes with which she was accused, and of which her Beauty, her Elegance, and her Sprightliness were sufficient proofs, not to mention her solemn Protestations of Innocence, the weakness of the Charges against her, and the King's Character; all of which add some confirmation, tho' perhaps but slight ones when in comparison with those before alledged in her favour. Tho' I do not profess giving many dates, yet as I think it proper to give some and shall of course make choice of those which it is most necessary for the Reader to know, I think it right to inform him that her letter to the King was dated on the 6th of May. The Crimes and Cruelties of this Prince, were too numerous to be mentioned, (as this history I trust has fully shown;) and nothing can be said in his vindication, but that his abolishing Religious Houses and leaving them to the ruinous depredations of time has been of infinite use to the landscape of England in general, which probably was a principal motive for his doing it, since otherwise why should a Man who was of no Religion himself be at so much trouble to abolish one which had for ages been established in the Kingdom. His Majesty's 5th Wife was the Duke of Norfolk's Neice who, tho' universally acquitted of the crimes for which she was beheaded, has been by many people supposed to have led an abandoned life before her Marriage—of this however I have many doubts, since she was a relation of that noble Duke of Norfolk who was so warm in the Queen of Scotland's cause, and who at last fell a victim to it. The Kings last wife contrived to survive him, but with difficulty effected it. He was succeeded by his only son Edward.

EDWARD the 6th

As this prince was only nine years old at the time of his Father's death, he was considered by many people as too young to govern, and the late King happening to be of the same opinion, his mother's Brother the Duke of Somerset was chosen Protector of the realm during his minority. This Man was on the whole of a very amiable Character, and is somewhat of a favourite with me, tho' I would by no means pretend to affirm that he was equal to those first of Men Robert Earl of Essex, Delamere, or Gilpin. He was beheaded, of which he might with reason have been proud, had he known that such was the death of Mary Queen of Scotland; but as it was impossible that he should be conscious of what had never happened, it does not appear that he felt particularly delighted with the manner of it. After his decease the Duke of Northumberland had the care of the King and the Kingdom, and

LOVE
AND
FREINDSHIP
AND
OTHER
EARLY
WORKS

performed his trust of both so well that the King died and the Kingdom was left to his daughter in law the Lady Jane Grey, who has been already mentioned as reading Greek. Whether she really understood that language or whether such a study proceeded only from an excess of vanity for which I beleive she was always rather remarkable, is uncertain. Whatever might be the cause, she preserved the same appearance of knowledge, and contempt of what was generally esteemed pleasure, during the whole of her life, for she declared herself displeased with being appointed Queen, and while conducting to the scaffold, she wrote a sentence in Latin and another in Greek on seeing the dead Body of her Husband accidentally passing that way.

MARY

This woman had the good luck of being advanced to the throne of England, in spite of the superior pretensions, Merit, and Beauty of her Cousins Mary Queen of Scotland and Jane Grey. Nor can I pity the Kingdom for the misfortunes they experienced during her Reign, since they fully deserved them, for having allowed her to succeed her Brother—which was a double peice of folly, since they might have foreseen that as she died without children, she would be succeeded by that disgrace to humanity, that pest of society, Elizabeth. Many were the people who fell martyrs to the protestant Religion during her reign; I suppose not fewer than a dozen. She married Philip King of Spain who in her sister's reign was famous for building Armadas. She died without issue, and then the dreadful moment came in which the destroyer of all comfort, the deceitful Betrayer of trust reposed in her, and the Murderess of her Cousin succeeded to the Throne.

ELIZABETH

It was the peculiar misfortune of this Woman to have bad Ministers—- Since wicked as she herself was, she could not have committed such extensive mischeif, had not these vile and abandoned Men connived at, and encouraged her in her Crimes. I know that it has by many people been asserted and beleived that Lord Burleigh, Sir Francis Walsingham, and the rest of those who filled the cheif offices of State were deserving, experienced, and able Ministers. But oh! how blinded such writers and such Readers must be to true Merit, to Merit despised, neglected and defamed, if they can persist in such opinions when they reflect that these men, these boasted men were such scandals to their Country and their sex as to allow and assist their Queen in confining for the space of nineteen years, a WOMAN who if the claims of Relationship and Merit were of no avail, yet as a Queen and as one who condescended to place confidence in her, had every reason to expect assistance and protection; and at length in allowing Elizabeth to bring this amiable Woman to an untimely, unmerited, and scandalous Death. Can any one if he reflects but for a moment on this blot, this everlasting blot upon their understanding and their Character, allow any praise to Lord Burleigh or Sir Francis Walsingham? Oh! what must this bewitching Princess whose only freind was then the Duke of Norfolk, and whose only ones now Mr Whitaker, Mrs Lefroy, Mrs Knight and myself, who was abandoned by her son, confined by her Cousin, abused, reproached and vilified by all, what must not her most noble mind have suffered when informed that Elizabeth had given orders for her Death! Yet she bore it with a most unshaken fortitude, firm in her mind; constant in her Religion; and prepared herself to meet the cruel fate to which she was doomed, with a magnanimity that would alone proceed from conscious Innocence. And yet could you Reader have beleived it possible that some hardened and zealous Protestants have even abused her for that steadfastness in the Catholic Religion which reflected on her so much credit? But this is a striking proof of THEIR narrow souls and prejudiced Judgements who accuse her. She was executed in the Great Hall at Fortheringay Castle (sacred Place!) on Wednesday the 8th of February 1586—to the everlasting Reproach of Elizabeth, her Ministers, and of England in general. It may not be unnecessary before I entirely conclude my account of this ill-fated Queen, to observe that she had been accused of several crimes during the time of her reigning in Scotland, of which I now most seriously do assure my Reader that she was entirely innocent; having never been guilty of anything more than Imprudencies into which she was betrayed by the openness of her Heart, her Youth, and her Education. Having I trust by this assurance entirely done away every Suspicion and every doubt which might have arisen in the Reader's mind, from what other Historians have written of her, I shall proceed to mention the remaining Events that marked Elizabeth's reign. It was about this time that Sir Francis Drake the first English Navigator who sailed round the World, lived, to be the ornament of his Country and his profession. Yet great as he was, and justly celebrated as a sailor, I cannot help foreseeing that he will be equalled in this or the next Century by one who tho' now but young, already promises to answer all the ardent and sanguine expectations of his Relations and Freinds, amongst whom I may class the amiable Lady to whom this work is dedicated, and my no less amiable self.

LOVE
AND
FREINDSHIP
AND
OTHER
EARLY
WORKS

Though of a different profession, and shining in a different sphere of Life, yet equally conspicuous in the Character of an Earl, as Drake was in that of a Sailor, was Robert Devereux Lord Essex. This unfortunate young Man was not unlike in character to that equally unfortunate one FREDERIC DELAMERE. The simile may be carried still farther, and Elizabeth the torment of Essex may be compared to the Emmeline of Delamere. It would be endless to recount the misfortunes of this noble and gallant Earl. It is sufficient to say that he was beheaded on the 25th of Feb, after having been Lord Lieutenant of Ireland, after having clapped his hand on his sword, and after performing many other services to his Country. Elizabeth did not long survive his loss, and died so miserable that were it not an injury to the memory of Mary I should pity her.

JAMES the 1st

Though this King had some faults, among which and as the most principal, was his allowing his Mother's death, yet considered on the whole I cannot help liking him. He married Anne of Denmark, and had several Children; fortunately for him his eldest son Prince Henry died before his father or he might have experienced the evils which befell his unfortunate Brother.

As I am myself partial to the roman catholic religion, it is with infinite regret that I am obliged to blame the Behaviour of any Member of it: yet Truth being I think very excusable in an Historian, I am necessitated to say that in this reign the roman Catholics of England did not behave like Gentlemen to the protestants. Their Behaviour indeed to the Royal Family and both Houses of Parliament might justly be considered by them as very uncivil, and even Sir Henry Percy tho' certainly the best bred man of the party, had none of that general politeness which is so universally pleasing, as his attentions were entirely confined to Lord Mounteagle.

Sir Walter Raleigh flourished in this and the preceeding reign, and is by many people held in great veneration and respect—But as he was an enemy of the noble Essex, I have nothing to say in praise of him, and must refer all those who may wish to be acquainted with the particulars of his life, to Mr Sheridan's play of the Critic, where they will find many interesting anecdotes as well of him as of his friend Sir Christopher Hatton.—His Majesty was of that amiable disposition which inclines to Freindship, and in such points was possessed of a keener penetration in discovering Merit than many other people. I once heard an excellent Sharade on a Carpet, of which the subject I am now on reminds me, and as I think it may afford my Readers some amusement to *find it out*, I shall here take the liberty of presenting it to them.

Sharade My first is what my second was to King James the 1st, and you tread on my whole.

The principal favourites of his Majesty were Car, who was afterwards created Earl of Somerset and whose name perhaps may have some share in the above mentioned Sharade, and George Villiers afterwards Duke of Buckingham. On his Majesty's death he was succeeded by his son Charles.

CHARLES the 1st

This amiable Monarch seems born to have suffered misfortunes equal to those of his lovely Grandmother; misfortunes which he could not deserve since he was her descendant. Never certainly were there before so many detestable Characters at one time in England as in this Period of its History; never were amiable men so scarce. The number of them throughout the whole Kingdom amounting only to *five*, besides the inhabitants of Oxford who were always loyal to their King and faithful to his interests. The names of this noble five who never forgot the duty of the subject, or swerved from their attachment to his Majesty, were as follows—The King himself, ever stedfast in his own support—Archbishop Laud, Earl of Strafford, Viscount Faulkland and Duke of Ormond, who were scarcely less strenuous or zealous in the cause. While the *villians* of the time would make too long a list to be written or read; I shall therefore content myself with mentioning the leaders of the Gang. Cromwell, Fairfax, Hampden, and Pym may be considered as the original Causers of all the disturbances, Distresses, and Civil Wars in which England for many years was embroiled. In this reign as well as in that of Elizabeth, I am obliged in spite of my attachment to the Scotch, to consider them as equally guilty with the generality of the English, since they dared to think differently from their Sovereign, to forget the Adoration which as *Stuarts* it was their Duty to pay them, to rebel against, dethrone and imprison the unfortunate Mary; to oppose, to deceive, and to sell the no less unfortunate Charles. The Events of this Monarch's reign are too numerous for my pen, and indeed the recital of any Events (except what I make myself) is uninteresting to me; my principal reason for undertaking the History of England being to Prove the innocence of the Queen of Scotland, which I flatter myself with having effectually done, and to abuse Elizabeth, tho' I am rather fearful of having fallen short in the latter part of my scheme. —As therefore it is not my intention to give any particular account of the

LOVE
AND
FREINDSHIP
AND
OTHER
EARLY
WORKS

distresses into which this King was involved through the misconduct and Cruelty of his Parliament, I shall satisfy myself with vindicating him from the Reproach of Arbitrary and tyrannical Government with which he has often been charged. This, I feel, is not difficult to be done, for with one argument I am certain of satisfying every sensible and well disposed person whose opinions have been properly guided by a good Education—and this Argument is that he was a *Stuart*.

Finis
Saturday Nov 26th 1791

A COLLECTION OF LETTERS

To Miss COOPER, COUSIN

Conscious of the Charming Character which in every Country, and every Clime in Christendom is Cried, Concerning you, with Caution and Care I Commend to your Charitable Criticism this Clever Collection of Curious Comments, which have been Carefully Culled, Collected and Classed by your Comical Cousin

The Author.

•

LETTER the FIRST From a MOTHER to her FREIND.

My Children begin now to claim all my attention in different Manner from that in which they have been used to receive it, as they are now arrived at that age when it is necessary for them in some measure to become conversant with the World, My Augusta is 17 and her sister scarcely a twelvemonth younger. I flatter myself that their education has been such as will not disgrace their appearance in the World, and that *they* will not disgrace their Education I have every reason to beleive. Indeed they are sweet Girls—. Sensible yet unaffected—Accomplished yet Easy—. Lively yet Gentle—. As their progress in every thing they have learnt has been always the same, I am willing to forget the difference of age, and to introduce them together into Public. This very Evening is fixed on as their first *entree* into Life, as we are to drink tea with Mrs Cope and her Daughter. I am glad that we are to meet no one, for my Girls sake, as it would be awkward for them to enter too wide a Circle on the very first day. But we shall proceed by degrees.—Tomorrow Mr Stanly's family will drink tea with us, and perhaps the Miss Phillips's will meet them. On Tuesday we shall pay Morning Visits—On Wednesday we are to dine at Westbrook. On Thursday we have Company at home. On Friday we are to be at a Private Concert at Sir John Wynna's—and on Saturday we expect Miss Dawson to call in the Morning—which will complete my Daughters Introduction into Life. How they will bear so much dissipation I cannot imagine; of their spirits I have no fear, I only dread their health.

This mighty affair is now happily over, and my Girls are *out*. As the moment approached for our departure, you can have no idea how the sweet Creatures trembled with fear and expectation. Before the Carriage drove to the door, I called them into my dressing-room, and as soon as they were seated thus addressed them. "My dear Girls the moment is now arrived when I am to reap the rewards of all my Anxieties and Labours towards you during your Education. You are this Evening to enter a World in which you will meet with many wonderfull Things; Yet let me warn you against suffering yourselves to be meanly swayed by the Follies and Vices of others, for beleive me my beloved Children that if you do—I shall be very sorry for it." They both assured me that they would ever remember my advice with Gratitude, and follow it with attention; That they were prepared to find a World full of things to amaze and to shock them: but that they trusted their behaviour would never give me reason to repent the Watchful Care with which I had presided over their infancy and formed their Minds—" "With such expectations and such intentions (cried I) I can have nothing to fear from you—and can chearfully conduct you to Mrs Cope's without a fear of your being seduced by her Example, or contaminated by her Follies. Come, then my Children (added I) the Carriage is driving to the door, and I will not a moment delay the happiness you are so impatient to enjoy." When we arrived at Warleigh, poor Augusta could scarcely breathe, while Margaret was all Life and Rapture. "The long-expected Moment is now arrived (said she) and we shall soon be in the World."—In a few Moments we were in Mrs Cope's parlour, where with her daughter she sate ready to receive us. I observed with delight the impression

LOVE
AND
FREINDSHIP
AND
OTHER
EARLY
WORKS

my Children made on them—. They were indeed two sweet, elegant-looking Girls, and tho' somewhat abashed from the peculiarity of their situation, yet there was an ease in their Manners and address which could not fail of pleasing—. Imagine my dear Madam how delighted I must have been in beholding as I did, how attentively they observed every object they saw, how disgusted with some Things, how enchanted with others, how astonished at all! On the whole however they returned in raptures with the World, its Inhabitants, and Manners.

Yrs Ever—A. F.

•

LETTER the SECOND From a YOUNG LADY crossed in Love to her freind

Why should this last disappointment hang so heavily on my spirits? Why should I feel it more, why should it wound me deeper than those I have experienced before? Can it be that I have a greater affection for Willoughby than I had for his amiable predecessors? Or is it that our feelings become more acute from being often wounded? I must suppose my dear Belle that this is the Case, since I am not conscious of being more sincerely attached to Willoughby than I was to Neville, Fitzowen, or either of the Crawfords, for all of whom I once felt the most lasting affection that ever warmed a Woman's heart. Tell me then dear Belle why I still sigh when I think of the faithless Edward, or why I weep when I behold his Bride, for too surely this is the case—. My Freinds are all alarmed for me; They fear my declining health; they lament my want of spirits; they dread the effects of both. In hopes of releiving my melancholy, by directing my thoughts to other objects, they have invited several of their freinds to spend the Christmas with us. Lady Bridget Darkwood and her sister-in-law, Miss Jane are expected on Friday; and Colonel Seaton's family will be with us next week. This is all most kindly meant by my Uncle and Cousins; but what can the presence of a dozen indefferent people do to me, but weary and distress me—. I will not finish my Letter till some of our Visitors are arrived.

Friday Evening Lady Bridget came this morning, and with her, her sweet sister Miss Jane—. Although I have been acquainted with this charming Woman above fifteen Years, yet I never before observed how lovely she is. She is now about 35, and in spite of sickness, sorrow and Time is more blooming than I ever saw a Girl of 17. I was delighted with her, the moment she entered the house, and she appeared equally pleased with me, attaching herself to me during the remainder of the day. There is something so sweet, so mild in her Countenance, that she seems more than Mortal. Her Conversation is as bewitching as her appearance; I could not help telling her how much she engaged my admiration—. "Oh! Miss Jane" (said I)—and stopped from an inability at the moment of expressing myself as I could wish—"Oh! Miss Jane"—(I repeated)—I could not think of words to suit my feelings—She seemed waiting for my speech—. I was confused—distressed—my thoughts were bewildered—and I could only add—"How do you do?" She saw and felt for my Embarrassment and with admirable presence of mind relieved me from it by saying—"My dear Sophia be not uneasy at having exposed yourself—I will turn the Conversation without appearing to notice it." Oh! how I loved her for her kindness! "Do you ride as much as you used to do?" said she—. "I am advised to ride by my Physician. We have delightful Rides round us, I have a Charming horse, am uncommonly fond of the Amusement, replied I quite recovered from my Confusion, and in short I ride a great deal." "You are in the right my Love," said she. Then repeating the following line which was an extempore and equally adapted to recommend both Riding and Candour—

"Ride where you may, Be Candid where you can," she added," I rode once, but it is many years ago—She spoke this in so low and tremulous a Voice, that I was silent—. Struck with her Manner of speaking I could make no reply. "I have not ridden, continued she fixing her Eyes on my face, since I was married." I was never so surprised—"Married, Ma'am!" I repeated. "You may well wear that look of astonishment, said she, since what I have said must appear improbable to you—Yet nothing is more true than that I once was married."

"Then why are you called Miss Jane?"

"I married, my Sophia without the consent or knowledge of my father the late Admiral Annesley. It was therefore necessary to keep the secret from him and from every one, till some fortunate opportunity might offer of revealing it—. Such an opportunity alas! was but too soon given in the death of my dear Capt. Dashwood—Pardon these tears, continued Miss Jane wiping her Eyes, I owe them to my Husband's memory. He fell my Sophia, while fighting for his Country in America after a most happy Union of seven years—. My Children, two sweet Boys and a Girl, who had constantly resided with my Father and me, passing with him and with every one as the Children of a Brother (tho' I had ever been an only Child) had as yet been the comforts of my Life. But no sooner had I lossed my Henry, than these sweet Creatures fell sick and died—. Conceive dear Sophia what my feelings must have been when as an Aunt I attended my Children to their early Grave—. My Father did not survive them many weeks—He died, poor Good old man, happily ignorant to his last hour of my Marriage."

"But did not you own it, and assume his name at your husband's death?"

"No; I could not bring myself to do it; more especially when in my Children I lost all inducement for doing it. Lady Bridget, and yourself are the only persons who are in the knowledge of my having ever been either Wife or Mother. As I could not Prevail on myself to take the name of Dashwood (a name which after my Henry's death I could never hear without emotion) and as I was conscious of having no right to that of Annesley, I dropt all thoughts of either, and have made it a point of bearing only my Christian one since my Father's death." She paused—"Oh! my dear Miss Jane (said I) how infinitely am I obliged to you for so entertaining a story! You cannot think how it has diverted me! But have you quite done?"

"I have only to add my dear Sophia, that my Henry's elder Brother dieing about the same time, Lady Bridget became a Widow like myself, and as we had always loved each other in idea from the high Character in which we had ever been spoken of, though we had never met, we determined to live together. We wrote to one another on the same subject by the same post, so exactly did our feeling and our actions coincide! We both eagerly embraced the proposals we gave and received of becoming one family, and have from that time lived together in the greatest affection."

"And is this all? said I, I hope you have not done."

"Indeed I have; and did you ever hear a story more pathetic?"

"I never did—and it is for that reason it pleases me so

much, for when one is unhappy nothing is so delightful to one's sensations as to hear of equal misery."

"Ah! but my Sophia why are YOU unhappy?"

"Have you not heard Madam of Willoughby's Marriage?"

"But my love why lament HIS perfidy, when you bore so well that of many young Men before?"

"Ah! Madam, I was used to it then, but when Willoughby broke his Engagements I had not been dissaopinted for half a year."

"Poor Girl!" said Miss Jane.

●

LETTER the THIRD From a YOUNG LADY in distressed Circumstances to her freind

A few days ago I was at a private Ball given by Mr Ashburnham. As my Mother never goes out she entrusted me to the care of Lady Greville who did me the honour of calling for me in her way and of allowing me to sit forwards, which is a favour about which I am very indifferent especially as I know it is considered as confering a great obligation on me "So Miss Maria (said her Ladyship as she saw me advancing to the door of the Carriage) you seem very smart to night—MY poor Girls will appear quite to disadvantage by YOU—I only hope your Mother may not have distressed herself to set YOU off. Have you got a new Gown on?"

"Yes Ma'am." replied I with as much indifference as I could assume.

"Aye, and a fine one too I think—(feeling it, as by her permission I seated myself by her) I dare say it is all very smart—But I must own, for you know I always speak my mind, that I think it was quite a needless piece of expence—Why could not you have worn your old striped one? It is not my way to find fault with People because they are poor, for I always think that they are more to be despised and pitied than blamed for it, especially if they cannot help it, but at the same time I must say that in my opinion your old striped Gown would have been quite fine enough for its Wearer—for to tell you the truth (I always speak my mind) I am very much afraid that one half of the people in the room will not know whether you have a Gown on or not—But I suppose you intend

LOVE
AND
FREINDSHIP
AND
OTHER
EARLY
WORKS

to make your fortune to night—. Well, the sooner the better; and I wish you success."

"Indeed Ma'am I have no such intention—"

"Who ever heard a young Lady own that she was a Fortune-hunter?" Miss Greville laughed but I am sure Ellen felt for me.

"Was your Mother gone to bed before you left her?" said her Ladyship.

"Dear Ma'am, said Ellen it is but nine o'clock."

"True Ellen, but Candles cost money, and Mrs Williams is too wise to be extravagant."

"She was just sitting down to supper Ma'am."

"And what had she got for supper?" "I did not observe." "Bread and Cheese I suppose." "I should never wish for a better supper." said Ellen. "You have never any reason replied her Mother, as a better is always provided for you." Miss Greville laughed excessively, as she constantly does at her Mother's wit.

Such is the humiliating Situation in which I am forced to appear while riding in her Ladyship's Coach—I dare not be impertinent, as my Mother is always admonishing me to be humble and patient if I wish to make my way in the world. She insists on my accepting every invitation of Lady Greville, or you may be certain that I would never enter either her House, or her Coach with the disagreable certainty I always have of being abused for my Poverty while I am in them.— When we arrived at Ashburnham, it was nearly ten o'clock, which was an hour and a half later than we were desired to be there; but Lady Greville is too fashionable (or fancies herself to be so) to be punctual. The Dancing however was not begun as they waited for Miss Greville. I had not been long in the room before I was engaged to dance by Mr Bernard, but just as we were going to stand up, he recollected that his Servant had got his white Gloves, and immediately ran out to fetch them. In the mean time the Dancing began and Lady Greville in passing to another room went exactly before me—She saw me and instantly stopping, said to me though there were several people close to us,

"Hey day, Miss Maria! What cannot you get a partner? Poor Young Lady! I am afraid your new Gown was put on for nothing. But do not despair; perhaps you may get a hop before the Evening is over." So saying, she passed on without hearing my repeated assurance of being engaged, and leaving me very much provoked at being so exposed before every one—Mr Bernard however soon returned and by coming to me the moment he entered the room, and leading me to the Dancers my Character I hope was cleared from the imputation Lady Greville had thrown on it, in the eyes of all the old Ladies who had heard her speech. I soon forgot all my vexations in the pleasure of dancing and of having the most agreable partner in the room. As he is moreover heir to a very large Estate I could see that Lady Greville did not look very well pleased when she found who had been his Choice—She was determined to mortify me, and accordingly when we were sitting down between the dances, she came to me with more than her usual insulting importance attended by Miss Mason and said loud enough to be heard by half the people in the room, "Pray Miss Maria in what way of business was your Grandfather? for Miss Mason and I cannot agree whether he was a Grocer or a Bookbinder." I saw that she wanted to mortify me, and was resolved if I possibly could to Prevent her seeing that her scheme succeeded. "Neither Madam; he was a Wine Merchant." "Aye, I knew he was in some such low way—He broke did not he?" "I beleive not Ma'am." "Did not he abscond?" "I never heard that he did." "At least he died insolvent?" "I was never told so before." "Why, was not your *father* as poor as a Rat" "I fancy not." "Was not he in the Kings Bench once?" "I never saw him there." She gave me *such* a look, and turned away in a great passion; while I was half delighted with myself for my impertinence, and half afraid of being thought too saucy. As Lady Greville was extremely angry with me, she took no further notice of me all the Evening, and indeed had I been in favour I should have been equally neglected, as she was got into a Party of great folks and she never speaks to me when she can to anyone else. Miss Greville was with her Mother's party at supper, but Ellen preferred staying with the Bernards and me. We had a very pleasant Dance and as Lady G—slept all the way home, I had a very comfortable ride.

The next day while we were at dinner Lady Greville's Coach stopped at the door, for that is the time of day she generally contrives it should. She sent in a message by the servant to say that "she should not get out but that Miss Maria must come to the Coach-door, as she wanted to speak to her, and that she must make haste and come immediately—" "What an impertinent Message Mama!" said I—"Go Maria—" replied she—Accordingly I went and was obliged to stand there at

LOVE
AND
FREINDSHIP
AND
OTHER
EARLY
WORKS

her Ladyships pleasure though the Wind was extremely high and very cold.

"Why I think Miss Maria you are not quite so smart as you were last night—But I did not come to examine your dress, but to tell you that you may dine with us the day after tomorrow—Not tomorrow, remember, do not come tomorrow, for we expect Lord and Lady Clermont and Sir Thomas Stanley's family—There will be no occasion for your being very fine for I shant send the Carriage—If it rains you may take an umbrella—" I could hardly help laughing at hearing her give me leave to keep myself dry—"And pray remember to be in time, for I shant wait—I hate my Victuals over-done—But you need not come before the time—How does your Mother do? She is at dinner is not she?" "Yes Ma'am we were in the middle of dinner when your Ladyship came." "I am afraid you find it very cold Maria." said Ellen. "Yes, it is an horrible East wind—said her Mother—I assure you I can hardly bear the window down—But you are used to be blown about by the wind Miss Maria and that is what has made your Complexion so rudely and coarse. You young Ladies who cannot often ride in a Carriage never mind what weather you trudge in, or how the wind shews your legs. I would not have my Girls stand out of doors as you do in such a day as this. But some sort of people have no feelings either of cold or Delicacy—Well, remember that we shall expect you on Thursday at 5 o'clock—You must tell your Maid to come for you at night—There will be no Moon—and you will have an horrid walk home—My compts to Your Mother—I am afraid your dinner will be cold—Drive on—" And away she went, leaving me in a great passion with her as she always does.

Maria Williams.

•

LETTER the FOURTH From a YOUNG LADY rather impertinent to her freind

We dined yesterday with Mr Evelyn where we were introduced to a very agreable looking Girl his Cousin. I was extremely pleased with her appearance, for added to the charms of an engaging face, her manner and voice had something peculiarly interesting in them. So much so, that they inspired me with a great curiosity to know the history of her Life, who were her Parents, where she came from, and what had befallen her, for it was then only known that she was a relation of Mr Evelyn, and that her name was Grenville. In the evening a favourable opportunity offered to me of attempting at least to know what I wished to know, for every one played at Cards but Mrs Evelyn, My Mother, Dr Drayton, Miss Grenville and myself, and as the two former were engaged in a whispering Conversation, and the Doctor fell asleep, we were of necessity obliged to entertain each other. This was what I wished and being determined not to remain in ignorance for want of asking, I began the Conversation in the following Manner.

"Have you been long in Essex Ma'am?"

"I arrived on Tuesday."

"You came from Derbyshire?"

"No, Ma'am! appearing surprised at my question, from Suffolk." You will think this a good dash of mine my dear Mary, but you know that I am not wanting for Impudence when I have any end in veiw. "Are you pleased with the Country Miss Grenville? Do you find it equal to the one you have left?"

"Much superior Ma'am in point of Beauty." She sighed. I longed to know for why.

"But the face of any Country however beautiful said I, can be but a poor consolation for the loss of one's dearest Freinds." She shook her head, as if she felt the truth of what I said. My Curiosity was so much raised, that I was resolved at any rate to satisfy it.

"You regret having left Suffolk then Miss Grenville?" "Indeed I do." "You were born there I suppose?" "Yes Ma'am I was and passed many happy years there—"

"That is a great comfort—said I—I hope Ma'am that you never spent any unhappy one's there."

"Perfect Felicity is not the property of Mortals, and no one has a right to expect uninterrupted Happiness. —Some Misfortunes I have certainly met with."

"*What* Misfortunes dear Ma'am?" replied I, burning with impatience to know every thing. "*None* Ma'am I hope that have been the effect of any wilfull fault in me." "I dare say not Ma'am, and have no doubt but that any sufferings you may have experienced could arise only from the cruelties of Relations or the Errors of Freinds." She sighed—"You seem unhappy my dear Miss Grenville—Is it in my power to soften your Misfortunes?" "YOUR power Ma'am replied she extremely surprised; it is in NO ONES power to make me happy." She pronounced these words in so mournfull and solemn an accent, that for some time I had not courage to reply. I was actually silenced. I recovered myself however in a few moments and looking at her with all the affection I could, "My dear Miss Grenville said I, you appear extremely young—and may probably stand in need of some one's advice whose regard for you, joined to superior Age, perhaps superior Judgement might authorise her to give it. I am that person, and I now challenge you to accept the offer I make you of my Confidence and Freindship, in return to which I shall only ask for yours—"

"You are extremely obliging Ma'am—said she—and I am highly flattered by your attention to me—But I am in no difficulty, no doubt, no uncertainty of situation in which any advice can be wanted. Whenever I am however continued she brightening into a complaisant smile, I shall know where to apply."

I bowed, but felt a good deal mortified by such a repulse; still however I had not given up my point. I found that by the appearance of sentiment and Freindship nothing was to be gained and determined therefore to renew my attacks by Questions and suppositions. "Do you intend staying long in this part of England Miss Grenville?"

"Yes Ma'am, some time I beleive."

"But how will Mr and Mrs Grenville bear your absence?"

"They are neither of them alive Ma'am." This was an answer I did not expect—I was quite silenced, and never felt so awkward in my Life.

●

LETTER the FIFTH From a YOUNG LADY very much in love to her Freind

My Uncle gets more stingy, my Aunt more particular, and I more in love every day. What shall we all be at this rate by the end of the year! I had this morning the happiness of receiving the following Letter from my dear Musgrove.

Sackville St: Janry 7th It is a month to day since I first beheld my lovely Henrietta, and the sacred anniversary must and shall be kept in a manner becoming the day—by writing to her. Never shall I forget the moment when her Beauties first broke on my sight—No time as you well know can erase it from my Memory. It was at Lady Scudamores. Happy Lady Scudamore to live within a mile of the divine Henrietta! When the lovely Creature first entered the room, oh! what were my sensations? The sight of you was like the sight ofa wonderful fine Thing. I started—I gazed at her with admiration—She appeared every moment more Charming, and the unfortunate Musgrove became a captive to your Charms before I had time to look about me. Yes Madam, I had the happiness of adoring you, an happiness for which I cannot be too grateful. "What," said he to himself, "is Musgrove allowed to die for Henrietta? Enviable Mortal! and may he pine for her who is the object of universal admiration, who is adored by a Colonel, and toasted by a Baronet!" Adorable Henrietta how beautiful you are! I declare you are quite divine! You are more than Mortal. You are an Angel. You are Venus herself. In short Madam you are the prettiest Girl I ever saw in my Life—and her Beauty is encreased in her Musgroves Eyes, by permitting him to love her and allowing me to hope. And ah! Angelic Miss Henrietta Heaven is my witness how ardently I do hope for the death of your villanous Uncle and his abandoned Wife, since my fair one will not consent to be mine till their decease has placed her in affluence above what my fortune can procure—. Though it is an improvable Estate—. Cruel Henrietta to persist in such a resolution! I am at Present with my sister where I mean to continue till my own house which tho' an excellent one is at Present somewhat out of repair, is ready to receive me. Amiable princess of my Heart farewell—Of that Heart which trembles while it signs itself Your most ardent Admirer and devoted humble servt. T. Musgrove.

There is a pattern for a Love-letter Matilda! Did you ever read such a master-piece of Writing? Such sense, such sentiment, such purity of Thought, such flow of Language and such unfeigned Love in one sheet? No, never I can answer for it, since a Musgrove is not to be met with by every Girl. Oh! how I long to be with him! I intend to send him the following in answer to his Letter tomorrow.

My dearest Musgrove—. Words cannot express how happy your Letter made me; I thought I should have cried for joy, for I love you better than any body in the World. I think you the most amiable, and the handsomest Man in England, and so to be sure you are. I never read so sweet a Letter in my Life.

LOVE
AND
FREINDSHIP
AND
OTHER
EARLY
WORKS

Do write me another just like it, and tell me you are in love with me in every other line. I quite die to see you. How shall we manage to see one another? for we are so much in love that we cannot live asunder. Oh! my dear Musgrove you cannot think how impatiently I wait for the death of my Uncle and Aunt—If they will not Die soon, I beleive I shall run mad, for I get more in love with you every day of my Life.

How happy your Sister is to enjoy the pleasure of your Company in her house, and how happy every body in London must be because you are there. I hope you will be so kind as to write to me again soon, for I never read such sweet Letters as yours. I am my dearest Musgrove most truly and faithfully yours for ever and ever Henrietta Halton.

I hope he will like my answer; it is as good a one as I can write though nothing to his; Indeed I had always heard what a dab he was at a Love-letter. I saw him you know for the first time at Lady Scudamores—And when I saw her Ladyship afterwards she asked me how I liked her Cousin Musgrove?

"Why upon my word said I, I think he is a very handsome young Man."

"I am glad you think so replied she, for he is distractedly in love with you."

"Law! Lady Scudamore said I, how can you talk so ridiculously?"

"Nay, t'is very true answered she, I assure you, for he was in love with you from the first moment he beheld you."

"I wish it may be true said I, for that is the only kind of love I would give a farthing for—There is some sense in being in love at first sight."

"Well, I give you Joy of your conquest, replied Lady Scudamore, and I beleive it to have been a very complete one; I am sure it is not a contemptible one, for my Cousin is a charming young fellow, has seen a great deal of the World, and writes the best Love-letters I ever read."

This made me very happy, and I was excessively pleased with my conquest. However, I thought it was proper to give myself a few Airs—so I said to her—

"This is all very pretty Lady Scudamore, but you know that we young Ladies who are Heiresses must not throw ourselves away upon Men who have no fortune at all."

"My dear Miss Halton said she, I am as much convinced of that as you can be, and I do assure you that I should be the last person to encourage your marrying anyone who had not some pretensions to expect a fortune with you. Mr Musgrove is so far from being poor that he has an estate of several hundreds an year which is capable of great Improvement, and an excellent House, though at Present it is not quite in repair."

"If that is the case replied I, I have nothing more to say against him, and if as you say he is an informed young Man and can write a good Love-letter, I am sure I have no reason to find fault with him for admiring me, tho' perhaps I may not marry him for all that Lady Scudamore."

"You are certainly under no obligation to marry him answered her Ladyship, except that which love himself will dictate to you, for if I am not greatly mistaken you are at this very moment unknown to yourself, cherishing a most tender affection for him."

"Law, Lady Scudamore replied I blushing how can you think of such a thing?"

"Because every look, every word betrays it, answered she; Come my dear Henrietta, consider me as a freind, and be sincere with me—Do not you prefer Mr Musgrove to any man of your acquaintance?"

"Pray do not ask me such questions Lady Scudamore, said I turning away my head, for it is not fit for me to answer them."

"Nay my Love replied she, now you confirm my suspicions. But why Henrietta should you be ashamed to own a well-placed Love, or why refuse to confide in me?"

"I am not ashamed to own it; said I taking Courage. I do not refuse to confide in you or blush to say that I do love your cousin Mr Musgrove, that I am sincerely attached to him, for it is no disgrace to love a handsome Man. If he were plain indeed I might have had reason to be ashamed of a passion which must have been mean since the object would have been unworthy. But with such a figure and face, and such beautiful hair as your Cousin has, why should I blush to own that such superior merit has made an impression on me."

"My sweet Girl (said Lady Scudamore embracing me with great affection) what a delicate way of thinking you have in these matters, and what a quick discernment for one of your years! Oh! how I honour you for such Noble Sentiments!"

"Do you Ma'am said I; You are vastly obliging. But pray Lady Scudamore did your Cousin himself tell you of his affection for me I shall like him the better if he did, for what is a Lover without a Confidante?"

"Oh! my Love replied she, you were born for each other.

LOVE
AND
FREINDSHIP
AND
OTHER
EARLY
WORKS

Every word you say more deeply convinces me that your Minds are actuated by the invisible power of simpathy, for your opinions and sentiments so exactly coincide. Nay, the colour of your Hair is not very different. Yes my dear Girl, the poor despairing Musgrove did reveal to me the story of his Love—. Nor was I surprised at it—I know not how it was, but I had a kind of presentiment that he would be in love with you."

"Well, but how did he break it to you?"

"It was not till after supper. We were sitting round the fire together talking on indifferent subjects, though to say the truth the Conversation was cheifly on my side for he was thoughtful and silent, when on a sudden he interrupted me in the midst of something I was saying, by exclaiming in a most Theatrical tone—"Yes I'm in love I feel it now And Henrietta Halton has undone me."

"Oh! What a sweet way replied I, of declaring his Passion! To make such a couple of charming lines about me! What a pity it is that they are not in rhime!"

"I am very glad you like it answered she; To be sure there was a great deal of Taste in it. And are you in love with her, Cousin? said I. I am very sorry for it, for unexceptionable as you are in every respect, with a pretty Estate capable of Great improvements, and an excellent House tho' somewhat out of repair, yet who can hope to aspire with success to the adorable Henrietta who has had an offer from a Colonel and been toasted by a Baronet"—"*That* I have—" cried I. Lady Scudamore continued. "Ah dear Cousin replied he, I am so well convinced of the little Chance I can have of winning her who is adored by thousands, that I need no assurances of yours to make me more thoroughly so. Yet surely neither you or the fair Henrietta herself will deny me the exquisite Gratification of dieing for her, of falling a victim to her Charms. And when I am dead"—continued her—

"Oh Lady Scudamore, said I wiping my eyes, that such a sweet Creature should talk of dieing!"

"It is an affecting Circumstance indeed, replied Lady Scudamore." "When I am dead said he, let me be carried and lain at her feet, and perhaps she may not disdain to drop a pitying tear on my poor remains."

"Dear Lady Scudamore interrupted I, say no more on this affecting subject. I cannot bear it."

"Oh! how I admire the sweet sensibility of your Soul, and

as I would not for Worlds wound it too deeply, I will be silent."

"Pray go on." said I. She did so.

"And then added he, Ah! Cousin imagine what my transports will be when I feel the dear precious drops trickle on my face! Who would not die to haste such extacy! And when I am interred, may the divine Henrietta bless some happier Youth with her affection, May he be as tenderly attached to her as the hapless Musgrove and while HE crumbles to dust, May they live an example of Felicity in the Conjugal state!"

Did you ever hear any thing so pathetic? What a charming wish, to be lain at my feet when he was dead! Oh! what an exalted mind he must have to be capable of such a wish! Lady Scudamore went on.

"Ah! my dear Cousin" replied I to him, "such noble behaviour as this, must melt the heart of any woman however obdurate it may naturally be; and could the divine Henrietta but hear your generous wishes for her happiness, all gentle as is her mind, I have not a doubt but that she would pity your affection and endeavour to return it." "Oh! Cousin answered he, do not endeavour to raise my hopes by such flattering assurances. No, I cannot hope to please this angel of a Woman, and the only thing which remains for me to do, is to die." "True Love is ever desponding replied I, but I my dear Tom will give you even greater hopes of conquering this fair one's heart, than I have yet given you, by assuring you that I watched her with the strictest attention during the whole day, and could plainly discover that she cherishes in her bosom though unknown to herself, a most tender affection for you."

"Dear Lady Scudamore cried I, This is more than I ever knew!"

"Did not I say that it was unknown to yourself? I did not, continued I to him, encourage you by saying this at first, that surprise might render the pleasure still Greater." "No Cousin replied he in a languid voice, nothing will convince me that I can have touched the heart of Henrietta Halton, and if you are deceived yourself, do not attempt deceiving me." "In short my Love it was the work of some hours for me to Persuade the poor despairing Youth that you had really a preference for him; but when at last he could no longer deny the force of my arguments, or discredit what I told him, his transports, his Raptures, his Extacies are beyond my power to describe."

"Oh! the dear Creature, cried I, how passionately he loves

LOVE
AND
FREINDSHIP
AND
OTHER
EARLY
WORKS

me! But dear Lady Scudamore did you tell him that I was totally dependant on my Uncle and Aunt?"

"Yes, I told him every thing."

"And what did he say."

"He exclaimed with virulence against Uncles and Aunts; Accused the laws of England for allowing them to Possess their Estates when wanted by their Nephews or Neices, and wished *he* were in the House of Commons, that he might reform the Legislature, and rectify all its abuses."

"Oh! the sweet Man! What a spirit he has!" said I.

"He could not flatter himself he added, that the adorable Henrietta would condescend for his sake to resign those Luxuries and that splendor to which she had been used, and accept only in exchange the Comforts and Elegancies which his limited Income could afford her, even supposing that his house were in Readiness to receive her. I told him that it could not be expected that she would; it would be doing her an injustice to suppose her capable of giving up the power she now possesses and so nobly uses of doing such extensive Good to the poorer part of her fellow Creatures, merely for the gratification of you and herself."

"To be sure said I, I *am* very Charitable every now and then. And what did Mr Musgrove say to this?"

"He replied that he was under a melancholy necessity of owning the truth of what I said, and that therefore if he should be the happy Creature destined to be the Husband of the Beautiful Henrietta he must bring himself to wait, however impatiently, for the fortunate day, when she might be freed from the power of worthless Relations and able to bestow herself on him."

What a noble Creature he is! Oh! Matilda what a fortunate one I am, who am to be his Wife! My Aunt is calling me to come and make the pies, so adeiu my dear freind, and beleive me yours etc—

H. Halton.

Finis

THE FEMALE PHILOSOPHER

A LETTER

My Dear Louisa Your friend Mr Millar called upon us yesterday in his way to Bath, whither he is going for his health; two of his daughters were with him, but the eldest and the three Boys are with their Mother in Sussex. Though you have often told me that Miss Millar was remarkably handsome, you never mentioned anything of her Sisters' beauty; yet they are certainly extremely pretty. I'll give you their description.—Julia is eighteen; with a countenance in which Modesty, Sense and Dignity are happily blended, she has a form which at once presents you with Grace, Elegance and Symmetry. Charlotte who is just sixteen is shorter than her Sister, and though her figure cannot boast the easy dignity of Julia's, yet it has a pleasing plumpness which is in a different way as estimable. She is fair and her face is expressive sometimes of softness the most bewitching, and at others of Vivacity the most striking. She appears to have infinite Wit and a good humour unalterable; her conversation during the half hour they set with us, was replete with humourous sallies, Bonmots and repartees; while the sensible, the amiable Julia uttered sentiments of Morality worthy of a heart like her own. Mr Millar appeared to answer the character I had always received of him. My Father met him with that look of Love, that social Shake, and cordial kiss which marked his gladness at beholding an old and valued freind from whom thro' various circumstances he had been separated nearly twenty years. Mr Millar observed (and very justly too) that many events had befallen each during that interval of time, which gave occasion to the lovely Julia for making most sensible reflections on the many changes in their situation which so long a period had occasioned, on the advantages of some, and the disadvantages of others. From this subject she made a short digression to the instability of human pleasures and the uncertainty of their duration, which led her to observe that all earthly Joys must be imperfect. She was proceeding to illustrate this doctrine by examples from the Lives of great Men when the Carriage came to the Door and the amiable Moralist with her Father and Sister was obliged to depart; but not without a promise of spending five or six months with us on their return. We of course mentioned you, and I assure you that ample Justice was done to your Merits by all. "Louisa Clarke (said I) is in general a very pleasant Girl, yet sometimes her good humour is clouded by Peevishness, Envy and Spite. She neither wants Understanding or is without some pretensions to Beauty, but these are so very trifling, that the value she sets on her personal charms, and the adoration she expects them to be offered are at once a striking example of her vanity, her pride, and her folly." So said I, and to my opinion everyone added weight by the concurrence of their own.

Your affectionate
Arabella Smythe.

LOVE
AND
FREINDSHIP
AND
OTHER
EARLY
WORKS

THE FIRST ACT OF A COMEDY

CHARACTERS

Popgun
Maria
Charles
Pistolletta
Postilion
Hostess
Chorus of ploughboys
Cook
and
Strephon Chloe

SCENE—AN INN
ENTER Hostess, Charles, Maria, and Cook.

Hostess to Maria: If the gentry in the Lion should want beds, shew them number 9.

Maria: Yes Mistress. *EXIT Maria*

Hostess to Cook: If their Honours in the Moon ask for the bill of fare, give it them.

Cook: I wull, I wull. *EXIT Cook.*

Hostess to Charles: If their Ladyships in the Sun ring their Bell— answer it.

Charles: Yes Madam. *EXEUNT Severally.*

SCENE CHANGES TO THE MOON, and discovers Popgun and Pistoletta.

Pistoletta: Pray papa how far is it to London?

Popgun: My Girl, my Darling, my favourite of all my Children, who art the picture of thy poor Mother who died two months ago, with whom I am going to Town to marry to Strephon, and to whom I mean to bequeath my whole Estate, it wants seven Miles.

SCENE CHANGES TO THE SUN—

ENTER Chloe and a chorus of ploughboys.

Chloe: Where am I? At Hounslow—Where go I? To London—What to do? To be married—Unto whom? Unto Strephon. Who is he? A Youth. Then I will sing a song.

SONG I go to Town And when I come down, I shall be married to Streephon. And that to me will be fun.

Chorus: Be fun, be fun, be fun, And that to me will be fun.

ENTER Cook—Cook: Here is the bill of fare.

Chloe reads: 2 Ducks, a leg of beef, a stinking partridge, and a tart.— I will have the leg of beef and the partridge. EXIT Cook. And now I will sing another song.

SONG I am going to have my dinner, After which I shan't be thinner, I wish I had here Strephon For he would carve the partridge if it should be a tough one.

Chorus: Tough one, tough one, tough one For he would carve the partridge if it Should be a tough one. *EXIT Chloe and Chorus.—*

SCENE CHANGES TO THE INSIDE OF THE LION.

Enter Strephon and Postilion. Streph: You drove me from Staines to this place, from whence I mean to go to Town to marry Chloe. How much is your due?

Post: Eighteen pence.

Streph: Alas, my freind, I have but a bad guinea with which I mean to support myself in Town. But I will pawn to you an undirected Letter that I received from Chloe.

Post: Sir, I accept your offer.

END OF THE FIRST ACT.

LOVE
AND
FREINDSHIP
AND
OTHER
EARLY
WORKS

A LETTER from a YOUNG LADY, whose feelings being too strong for her Judgement led her into the commission of Errors which her Heart disapproved.

Many have been the cares and vicissitudes of my past life, my beloved Ellinor, and the only consolation I feel for their bitterness is that on a close examination of my conduct, I am convinced that I have strictly deserved them. I murdered my father at a very early period of my Life, I have since murdered my Mother, and I am now going to murder my Sister. I have changed my religion so often that at present I have not an idea of any left. I have been a perjured witness in every public tryal for these last twelve years; and I have forged my own Will. In short there is scarcely a crime that I have not committed—But I am now going to reform. Colonel Martin of the Horse guards has paid his Addresses to me, and we are to be married in a few days. As there is something singular in our Courtship, I will give you an account of it. Colonel Martin is the second son of the late Sir John Martin who died immensely rich, but bequeathing only one hundred thousand pound apeice to his three younger Children, left the bulk of his fortune, about eight Million to the present Sir Thomas. Upon his small pittance the Colonel lived tolerably contented for nearly four months when he took it into his head to determine on getting the whole of his eldest Brother's Estate. A new will was forged and the Colonel produced it in Court—but nobody would swear to it's being the right will except himself, and he had sworn so much that Nobody beleived him. At that moment I happened to be passing by the door of the Court, and was beckoned in by the Judge who told the Colonel that I was a Lady ready to witness anything for the cause of Justice, and advised him to apply to me. In short the Affair was soon adjusted. The Colonel and I swore to its' being the right will, and Sir Thomas has been obliged to resign all his illgotten wealth. The Colonel in gratitude waited on me the next day with an offer of his hand—. I am now going to murder my Sister.

Yours Ever,
Anna Parker.

LOVE
AND
FREINDSHIP
AND
OTHER
EARLY
WORKS

A TOUR THROUGH WALES—in a LETTER from a YOUNG LADY

My Dear Clara

I have been so long on the ramble that I have not till now had it in my power to thank you for your Letter—. We left our dear home on last Monday month; and proceeded on our tour through Wales, which is a principality contiguous to England and gives the title to the Prince of Wales. We travelled on horseback by preference. My Mother rode upon our little poney and Fanny and I walked by her side or rather ran, for my Mother is so fond of riding fast that she galloped all the way. You may be sure that we were in a fine perspiration when we came to our place of resting. Fanny has taken a great many Drawings of the Country, which are very beautiful, tho' perhaps not such exact resemblances as might be wished, from their being taken as she ran along. It would astonish you to see all the Shoes we wore out in our Tour. We determined to take a good Stock with us and therefore each took a pair of our own besides those we set off in. However we were obliged to have them both capped and heelpeiced at Carmarthen, and at last when they were quite gone, Mama was so kind as to lend us a pair of blue Sattin Slippers, of which we each took one and hopped home from Hereford delightfully.

I am your ever affectionate
Elizabeth Johnson.

A TALE

AGentleman whose family name I shall conceal, bought a small Cottage in Pembrokeshire about two years ago. This daring Action was suggested to him by his elder Brother who promised to furnish two rooms and a Closet for him, provided he would take a small house near the borders of an extensive Forest, and about three Miles from the Sea. Wilhelminus gladly accepted the offer and continued for some time searching after such a retreat when he was one morning agreably releived from his suspence by reading this advertisement in a Newspaper.

> TO BE LETT A Neat Cottage on the borders of an extensive forest and about three Miles from the Sea. It is ready furnished except two rooms and a Closet.

The delighted Wilhelminus posted away immediately to his brother, and shewed him the advertisement. Robertus congratulated him and sent him in his Carriage to take possession of the Cottage. After travelling for three days and six nights without stopping, they arrived at the Forest and following a track which led by it's side down a steep Hill over which ten Rivulets meandered, they reached the Cottage in half an hour. Wilhelminus alighted, and after knocking for some time without receiving any answer or hearing any one stir within, he opened the door which was fastened only by a wooden latch and entered a small room, which he immediately perceived to be one of the two that were unfurnished—From thence he proceeded into a Closet equally bare. A pair of stairs that went out of it led him into a room above, no less destitute, and these apartments he found composed the whole of the House. He was by no means displeased with this discovery, as he had the comfort of reflecting that he should not be obliged to lay out anything on furniture himself—. He returned immediately to his Brother, who took him the next day to every Shop in Town, and bought what ever was requisite to furnish the two rooms and the Closet, In a few days everything was completed, and Wilhelminus returned to take possession of his Cottage. Robertus accompanied him, with his Lady the amiable Cecilia and her two lovely Sisters Arabella and Marina to whom Wilhelminus was tenderly attached, and a large number of Attendants.—An ordinary Genius might probably have been embarrassed, in endeavouring to accomodate so large a party, but Wilhelminus with admirable presence of mind gave orders for the immediate erection of two noble Tents in an open spot in the Forest adjoining to the house. Their Construction was both simple and elegant—A couple of old blankets, each supported by four sticks, gave a striking proof of that taste for architecture and that happy ease in overcoming difficulties which were some of Wilhelminus's most striking Virtues.

LOVE
AND
FREINDSHIP
AND
OTHER
EARLY
WORKS

OH Editions Classic Library

This book is part of a range of highly designed fiction and non-fiction classics. With bold, eye-catching graphic covers by Evi-O.Studio, this collection aims to introduce a selection of the most-celebrated works of the last thousand years to a new audience. Featuring tales of adventure; fiction from the 19th and 20th centuries; feminist writings; and reflections on art, politics and philosophy, this is a small, wide-reaching and essential collection.

Evi-O.Studio is a design office specialising in publications, brand identity and creative collaborations. The studio is led by Evi O., a multi-disciplinary designer and artist. Over her 15 years creative odyssey, she has tailored award-winning publications that brought joy to readers and created colourful abstract art adorning homes of collectors. The studio is based in Marrickville, Sydney, servicing the world.

Published in 2022 by OH Editions
Part of Welbeck Publishing Group.
Based in London and Sydney.
www.welbeckpublishing.com

Design © 2022 OH Editions

A CIP catalogue record for this book is available from the British Library.

ISBN 978-1-80453-005-4
Publisher: Kate Pollard
Editor: Matt Tomlinson
Designer: Evi-O.Studio | Evi O, Emi Chiba & Susan Le
Production controller: Arlene Alexander

Printed and bound by Graficas Estella in Spain

10 9 8 7 6 5 4 3 2 1